THE TIME MASTERS

THE JON KIRK OF ARES CHRONICLES

The Winged Men
The Invisible Men
The Space Men
The Mind Masters
The Time Masters

THE TIME MASTERS

THE JON KIRK OF ARES CHRONICLES, BOOK FIVE

GARY LOVISI

*A Scientific Romance inspired by Edgar Rice Burroughs'
John Carter Series and set upon the faraway planet Ares*

WILDSIDE PRESS

Published by Wildside Press LLC.
www.wildsidebooks.com

CONTENTS

The People & Places in the Jon Kirk of Ares Chronicles 7

Chapter 1: *A Glitch in Time* 15

Chapter 2: *Earth in the Balance* 23

Chapter 3: *What Next?* 29

Chapter 4: *The Kin-Ty-Roo* 37

Chapter 5: *Battle Plan* 41

Chapter 6: *The Sacred Ku* 51

Chapter 7: *The Entity* 56

Chapter 8: *The Place of Meaning* 63

Chapter 9: *Options* 82

Chapter 10: *The Dark Tide* 89

Chapter 11: *The Turning Point* 101

Chapter 12: *The Thinking* 106

Chapter 13: *The Reason Is Made Clear* 115

Chapter 14: *A Treacherous Blade* 124

Chapter 15: *Still More Treachery* 130

Chapter 16: *And He Shall Meet His End* 137

Chapter 17: *To the End of Time* 146

Chapter 18: *The Mind Masters Go Home* 149

Chapter 19: *My Visit To Earth* 152

About the Author, Cover Artist, and Mapmaker 155

THE PEOPLE & PLACES IN THE JON KIRK OF ARES CHRONICLES

ALUN KIRK: the son of Emperor Jon Kirk and Lady Sirah of the Green Empire of Ares. At this time he is still a baby boy but he will become as great a warrior as his father.

AKAR: captain of the enemy space warship, *The Attara*, aka *The Destroyer*, who is defeated by Jon Kirk and then joins his forces.

ANCIENT BOOK OF KOR: a mythical lost tome said to possess the super-science of the ancient people of Ares.

ARON THE ELDEST: elder and mind-power master of the Old Ones of Keva. The leader of the Mind Masters.

AR-DEN: ancient wise man and one of Jon Kirk's most important counselors.

ATTARA, THE: warship in Lord Doom's fleet commanded by Captain Aka, a Gorm *consignat*. The ship name translates to *The Destroyer*.

BLACK DRAGONS, THE: mounted riders and warriors who are the body guard of Emperor Jon Kirk.

BLUE KORTAS: alien blue-skinned horned mercenaries, large mutant well armed killers not native to Ares and brought in to fight for The Secret Empire. Now allied with Jon Kirk under their leader General Zod.

BRAN: one of The Secret Empire prisoners and a pirate from the planet of Ko-Ah-Leh who befriends Jon Kirk.

CALIAT: one of the six green cities on the continent of Cos on the planet Ares occupied by the Zaran Winged-men and then set free by Jon Kirk and Tar-gool, renamed Tarcos in honor of Tar-gool.

CALI-NOR: a mystical realm or city that to the Greens of Ares most closely approximates their version of our Heaven.

CAVES OF CONSCIENCE: a huge network of caves north of Tarcos in the Coastal Mountains that Jon Kirk used as his headquarters during the invasion of Ares.

CAXIL: Gorm word for a dirty rat-like creature that lives on that planet, an insult.

CONSIGNATS: impressed fighters, or slaves, forced to fight for The Secret Empire of The Hundred Worlds.

DARK NIGHT: Flagship of Lord Protector Doom leader of The Secret Empire fleet in orbit around Ares.

DARK SPHERE, THE: the mind lands, or soul of all the people of Ares who have ever lived—a kind of universal mind in the Ares concept of Heaven, the Cali-Nor. It is dangerous to contact and difficult to control. Also known as The Sacred Ku.

DEATH RAY, THE: Ares space warship commanded by Gorm of the Gorms.

DAUNTLESS, THE: Jon Kirk's flagship of his three warship force that attacked three of Doom's warships. Captained by Kevnar, a female felina.

EMPTY QUARTER, THE: a vast void in the Known Universe where the entity called the Kin-Ty-Roo is located. An area of space where the entity has absorbed all suns, planets, and all matter.

FIGHTER, THE: Ares apace warship commanded by Tor-nul.

GENERAL ZOD: military leader of all Blue Korta empire shock troops.

GORM: of the Gorms, a large Viking-sized alien who befriends Jon Kirk.

HE WHO IS NOT TO BE NAMED: also known by the words Kin-Ty-Roo, said to be Emperor of the Known Universe and master of what is called The Enemy Empire, which is locked in a vicious war with The Secret Empire of The Hundred Worlds ruled by the Sindaki Lords.

HUNDRED WORLDERS: short name for minions of The Secret Empire of the Hundred Worlds, also known as The Secret Empire, ruled by the Sindaki Lords.

JON KIRK: Emperor of The Green Empire of The Six Cities of Ares and Earthman hero, husband to Empress Sirah, father of Alun Kirk.

KAL-SAR: Imperial governor of one of the Six Cities who defied Jon Kirk's order to evacuate his city and fought the Blue Kortas. His entire army and civilian population was massacred by the enemy.

KEV: hidden city on the western continent of Ares. See Keva.

KEVNAR: Captain of The Dauntless, a female felina and friend to Jon Kirk.

KEVA: ancient hidden city of the Greens whose people have great mind powers, destroyed by a ship of Lord Mentep's fleet and later rebuilt and renamed Kev in a secret location on the western continent of Ares.

KIN-TY-ROO: words to indicate the being called Emperor of the Known Universe, the words roughly translate into the phrase "He Who Is Not To be Named", but this being is a complete mystery but is master of what is called The Enemy Empire.

LARL: Mythical ancient Ares youth, son to hero Ry-Nar who entered the body of the dread Zarbane monster to retrieve his body.

LORD PROTECTOR KARLATH DOOM: Lord Protector and leader of the Secret Empire of the Hundred Worlds fleet in orbit around Ares. His flagship was *Dark Night*. Doom is a Sindaki, a race who is said to have unnatural mystical powers.

MANALIA: wife to Zaor, Jon Kirk's most trusted friend and general of the Green Empire army of Ares.

NEWCOMERS: general name of the minions of The Enemy Empire troops under the Kin-Ty-Roo or Emperor of The Known Universe.

PLACE OF MEANING, THE: the area within the Kin-Ty-Roo where control and purpose of the alien entity are ordered and where Jon Kirk fights the thing.

POLN: female *felina* tiger creature who befriends Jon Kirk.

QUARTO: Winged-man from Zar who is the captain of *Dark Night*, the flagship of Lord Protector Doom of The Secret Empire of the Hundred Worlds, later becomes Admiral Quarto-Zar of the fleet.

RAS-NOOR: Ares scientist, associate of the great Tar-gool, master scientist of Ares and the man whose machine brought Jon Kirk from Earth to Ares.

RY-NAR: Ancient Ares warrior hero who entered the dread monster Zarbane to retrieve the body of his son Larl, much in the manner of Jonah and the whale on Earth.

SACRED KU, THE: The mind residue of the souls of the departed of Ares, Sindalki and all the worlds of the Known Universe. A reservoir of vast power within what is called The Dark Sphere, a type of Universal Mind.

SAHN-JOR: friend of Jon Kirk and the First Minister and administrator of the Green Empire of Ares.

SECRET EMPIRE, THE: known as The Secret Empire of The Hundred Worlds, interplanetary empire of which the Winged-men from Zar are a part, a very small part, and which is seeking to reestablish Zaran rule on Ares and enslave the greens-skinned humans and destroy Jon Kirk and his Green Empire.

SHAMAR: young king of the mind-powerful people of Keva, later he is king of Kev, and a friend to Jon Kirk.

SHARN: Leader of the alien Tergats and sub-commander who runs the control room of the prison ship *Solar Happiness*, and who joined with Jon Kirk.

SASHEEN: merman from the sea world of Talu who befriended Jon Kirk.

SHORNS: a religious sect on Zar whose Winged-men adherents believe in peace and non-violence. They do not eat meat or people. Captain Quarto is a Shorns.

SIRAH: Empress of The Green Empire of Ares and wife to Earthman and Emperor Jon Kirk. Mother of Alun Kirk.

SLOSS: Ares word for garbage, or lies.

SOLAR HAPPINESS: prison ship of the Secret Empire captured by Jon Kirk and his companions.

SUNJOR: Ares military rank equivalent to corporal.

TAMBU: a Gorm from the planet Gorm who is a blood brother and companion to the huge Viking-like alien creature called Gorm.

TAR-GOOL: an old man, master scientist and patriot of the green-skinned humans of Ares, friend of Jon Kirk. He was killed in the battle to free the city of Caliat from the Zaran Winged-men, the city of Caliat was renamed Tarcos in his honor.

TAR-MEK: Black Dragon bodyguard who becomes controlled by the Kin-Ty-Roo and attempts to assassinate Jon Kirk.

TERGATS: race of tall, gangly yellow-skin humanoids with fins under control of the Secret Empire. Sharn is a leader of the Tergats.

THREE FORMS OF POWER, THE: The Ancient Ares philosophy of the three actions of warfare, encompassing the Physical, Super-science, and the power of the Mind Masters to defeat an enemy. Used by the Sindalki to take down the Ancients of Ares and to found The Secret Empire of The Hundred Worlds.

TOR-NUL: Captain of Emperor Jon Kirk's imperial bodyguard, the Black Dragons.

TRONTA: a young Keven who was stationed as the mind master on *The Dauntless*.

UNITED FEDERATION OF THE KNOWN UNIVERSE: The group of worlds and peoples in the Orion section of space that make up the old empire ruled by Jon Kirk, located in the area of space called by them as The Known Universe.

VUL-CAN: Ancient Ares colony world located between Mars and Jupiter, long ago destroyed by the Sindalki and now forming the Asteroid Belt.

WINGED-MEN: the brutal flying creatures from the planet Zar who have terrorized, murdered and eaten the green-skinned humans of Ares for millennia, also called Zarans.

ZAOR: Jon Kirk's most trusted captain and best friend on the planet Ares, brother of his wife, Sirah. General of the Green Empire army.

ZAR: home world of the Winged-men, one of the planets in the Orion star system.

ZARBANE: a mythical massive vicious monster of ancient Ares texts. Heroic Ry-Nar entered such a beast to retrieve his son Larl's body.

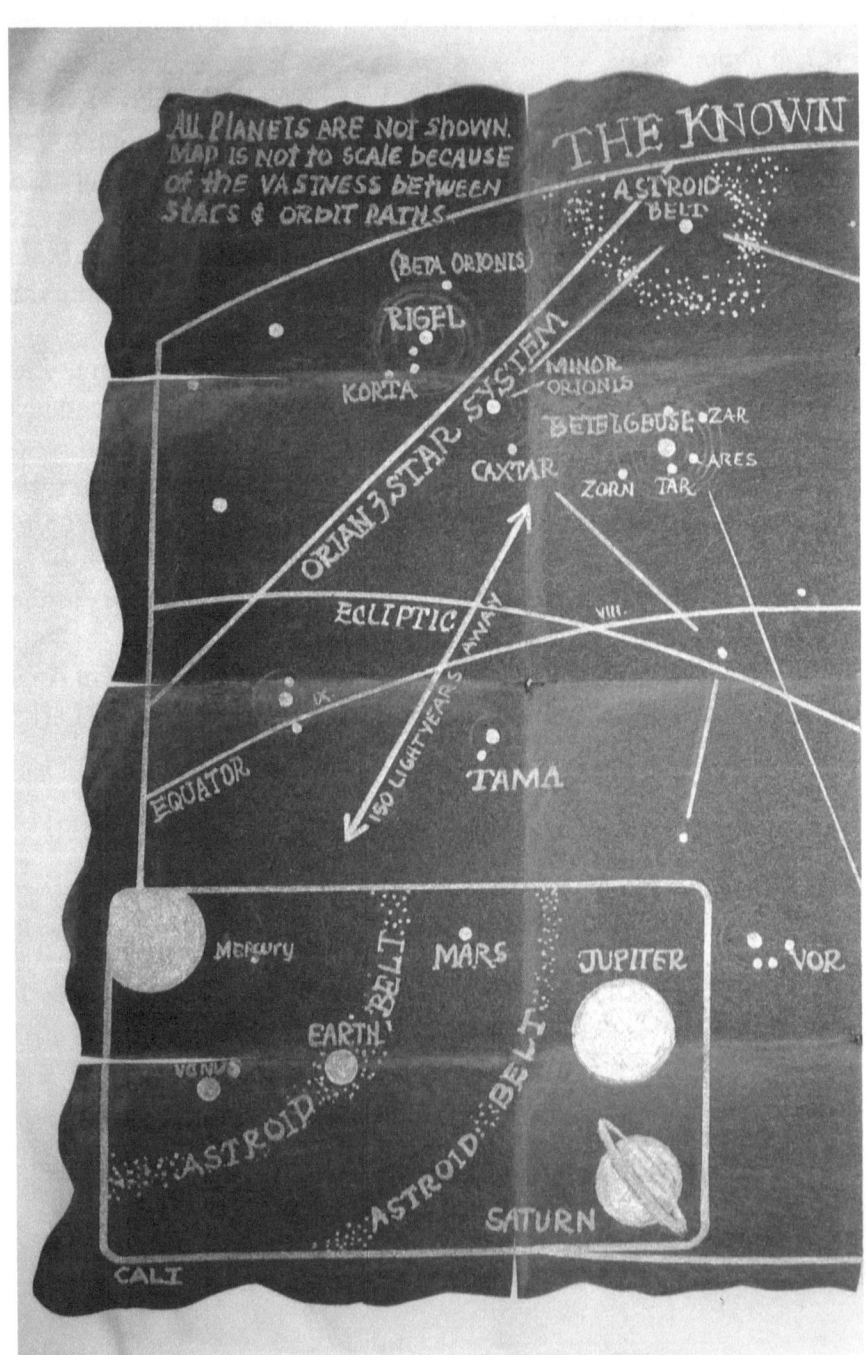

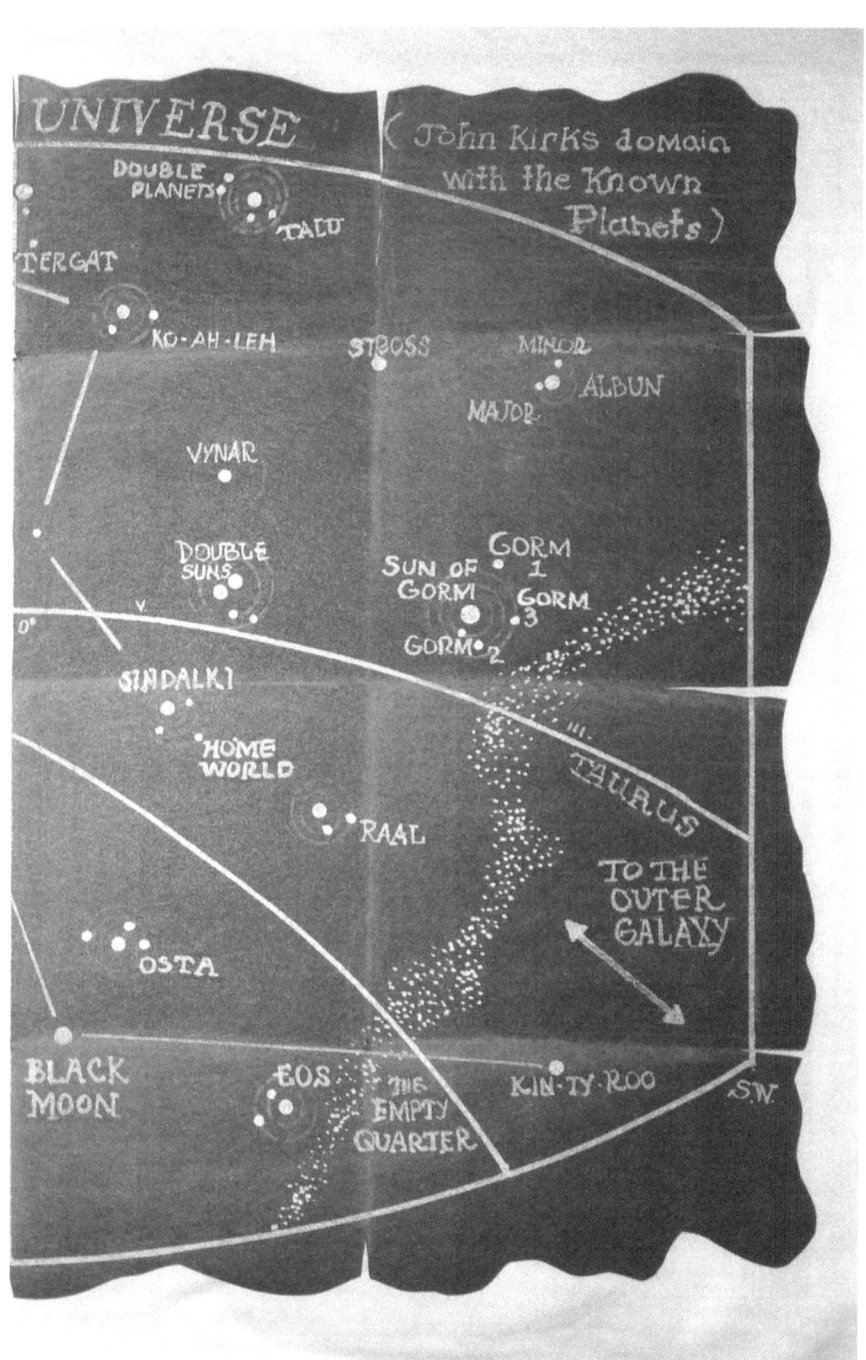

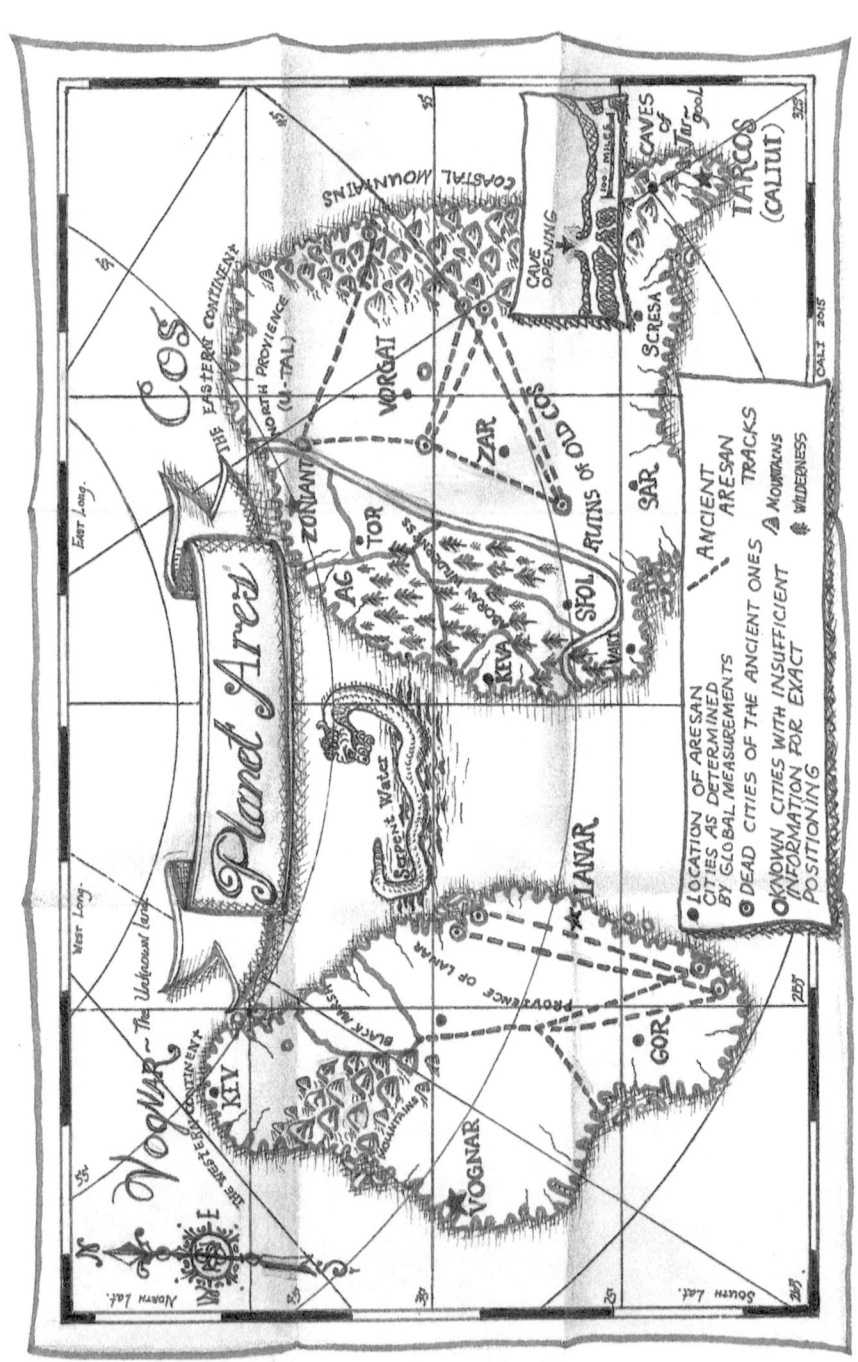

CHAPTER 1

A Glitch in Time

I felt like I was lost in another time, and another place. For some reason my thoughts reverted to my past life as a young boy growing up back on the Earth and I fondly recalled heroic classic western films and their strong stalwart heroes. Those were the action and adventure movies where the cowboys and the Indians fought bloody wars against each other in the classic American Wild West, and where the cavalry always seemed to come to the rescue just when they were needed—always in the nick of time. Or films where the brave heroic sheriff fought and defeated the outlaw or bank robber in a shoot-out on Main Street. I felt like I was playing that sheriff or cavalry role now—coming to the rescue of the Earth. I do not know why I had these thoughts circulating within my mind just then, but I recalled images of some of the great western heroes I had idolized as a youth; Errol Flynn, Gary Cooper, Clint Eastwood, and of course, John 'The Duke' Wayne. It was most strange, but somehow reassuring to have thoughts of them within my mind just then. Their bravery and honesty was dauntless. Their American can-do spirit was especially comforting. These men could achieve anything! I would be like them!

Regardless of these thoughts and images, and even though I knew I could not compare with those magnificent heroes at all, I allowed a grim smile when I thought of them. For I took solace from them and their heroic deeds, and I needed all the help I could get now. In truth, these fellows were not such a bad bunch of guys to want to emulate now that I found myself in such a dire situation as lay before me—and I was surely in a most dire situation. I knew I would need the heroic bravery and sheer luck I had seen demonstrated by these heroes of my childhood as I had never needed it before.

Lord Karlath Doom was dead. I had killed the demonic Sindalki lord in our present timeline—but back in the past where I was now going to be transported, he was still a formidable enemy—and he was very much alive!

I was about to embark upon a mission like no other I had ever encountered in my life. I looked at the stern face of the Keven mind master, Lord Aron, as he came over to me. He looked sad but determined.

I was only determined.

"We have prepared things here so that you will be transported through time and appear in the past, bare moments before Doom destroyed your Earth. It is a mere glitch in time for us, but it is all that it will take to send you back there. Once there, you must act fast, Jon Kirk. Kill Lord Doom at the precise moment immediately before he gives the order to destroy your Earth. The closer to that moment in time that he dies, the better the effect of your action will be to save your Earth," Aron The Eldest, leader of the Keven mind masters told me all this as I made myself ready for my most strange and dangerous of all transfer missions. For it was a mission that would propel me through time *and* space!

Ras-noor's scientists carefully strapped me into Tar-gool's ancient Ares projection machine, a most complicated device that would physically transport the image of my body to Earth. At the same time, the mind masters of Kev prepared to form a powerful mind meld with Lord Kneth instructing them. Through their talents and powers they would transport my physical image back into the past, to a time just moments before Lord Doom had destroyed the Earth.

It was weird and strange, but it seemed fairly cut and dry when it was explained to me, even though there was much that I did not fully understand about the procedure. I did know that everything had to be done very carefully, and every action had to coalesce together precisely at the same moment in time for me to be successful. Therein lied the rub. I deftly prepared my mind and thoughts for what was to come.

This plan seemed to me to be mostly based on theory and guesswork, as our mind masters had never actually performed time travel before, and it could prove to be deadly dangerous even if they were able to get me back into the past. This was an action I was not at all sure they could accomplish. I knew I was taking a big chance taking on this mission, but I had to do it. The possible benefit of saving Earth and its people far outweighed any dangers to myself. The danger could also be considerable to many other worlds if I caused some manner of time displacement, or created an error where I changed the past in some negative way. Time travel could be most complicated and allowed no room for error. It was deadly dangerous business, but I took my mission on willingly. For I would try anything to save the world of my birth. I did hope that if I ever did accomplish this mission, that I would be able to be brought home back to my own time and place here on Ares. They said that they thought they could do that too—bring me back home safely—after my mission was done. However, that was not a done deal either. So I had a lot on my mind just then, though I subordinated all my fears and thoughts to the success of the mission.

Crooch was there as well now. I caught him as he suddenly motioned to me quickly, drawing my attention. Crooch, the vilest of traitors, a man who had betrayed me many times in the past—but that was all in the past now as far as I was concerned. Our past. Now he and I were beyond that, and had entered a new and very different future—or so I hoped. For when it had proved most critical to us all, Crooch had been the one to set me free on Lord Doom's flagship, and he had fought against his other two companions, the wicked Tob and the sadist Vakon. He had fought both villains to the death. He had in fact done all this to protect me. He had saved me. He had released me and given me my freedom, and that had allowed me to meet Lord Doom in final personal combat and to defeat him and save Ares. We had won the battle of the black moon because of him.

And now I was going to save the Earth.

So what about Crooch? He stood there quietly and he looked at me meaningfully. The man was a mystery to me. He had been a man of no honor and abundant treachery. Could such a man change so completely? Was it even possible?

"What do you want, Crooch?" I asked him quickly as Ras-noor and his scientists readied the controls on their machine as they swarmed around me, and Lord Aron and his mind masters quickly worked to build their mind meld.

"Do it, save your world, Jon Kirk. If anyone can do it, you can," he told me in as friendly a tone as was possible for such as he. I was quite surprised by his words.

I gave him a slim grin and thanked him for his vote of confidence, but I knew this man, and I knew that he wanted something, so then I simply added in a low voice, "What is it you want, Crooch?"

"When you return, My Emperor. I shall ask you then," Crooch crooned softly. "Is that agreeable with you?"

I looked at him and just nodded, it seemed a moot point now. I might never return at all. I was getting ready to embark upon the most dangerous mission I had ever encountered since coming to Ares. It was a dangerous mission to save Earth from Lord Doom's destruction in our time's past. There was not a very good chance that I would accomplish that goal, and if so, there was no guarantee that I would be able to return to the here and now—my present time. Nevertheless, I still had a mission to perform and I would do it to the best of my ability. I had to save the Earth—if it was possible. I at least had to try. I would make it possible!

The machine hummed, then flashed a spark, shaking rather violently. I heard Lord Aron and the Keven mind masters humming in low voices as they took control of their mind meld, each one in a deep trance. That was the last thing I heard.

Suddenly everything changed around me.

Then everything was gone!

* * * *

I instantly found myself on Lord Doom's flagship where it was in high Earth orbit. I was on the bridge—or more accurately seemingly floating somewhere *above* the bridge and looking down upon it. I could see the ship's view screen with the Earth below me and the land mass of the United States visible. It looked lovely. Just as I remembered it. So calm, so peaceful, at least from way up here in orbit. I saw Lord Doom below me talking to an image that I now saw was an earlier version of myself from long ago. It was that past version of myself when I had been visiting my friend in his house down upon the Earth—when Doom had come there to threaten me and my world.

I looked carefully at Lord Doom—he did not seem to be able to detect my presence, and his ship's sensors did not alert him or his crew that I—or more accurately, my transported image—was there apparently floating in the upper area above his ship's bridge looking down upon them all. Doom's earlier version of himself appeared just as deadly as the version of him I had recently killed in my own present time—and now back in the past he looked just as deadly. I repressed a shudder to see that he was still alive here, and I would venture that he was just as deadly here as he ever was.

Lord Doom and I had a long tangled history. In fact, I had first killed Doom in my audience chamber in Tarcos back upon Ares many months ago, but almost immediately after that battle his dead body had regenerated in front of me and a room full of people to come back to life. He had been apparently undamaged by that supposed death. Then he had escaped vowing vengeance upon me.

I had killed Doom a second time—and this time it was for all eternity—mere days ago in our present time line. That had been in the darkness of the far away Empty Quarter of interstellar space while I had been held as a prisoner on his flagship and been set free by Crooch during the Battle at the Black Moon. That death I knew had been permanent. I made sure that it would be permanent.

So now Lord Doom was dead in my present time line—and had met his demise for all future time lines—and I hoped he would soon be dead in this past if I had anything to do about it. However, I was careful and concerned, for a victory by him here and now could cause my mission to fail—and that meant the permanent destruction of Earth and her entire population. It would also keep me from seeing my beloved Sirah, and Alun, ever again. And Ares would be in peril, with me unable to help. I would try to change all that from happening now.

I watched carefully as Lord Doom transported his image down to the planet below. I knew exactly where he was sending that image—even as the actual physical body of Doom was still standing in a thought transfer trance upon his ship's bridge. He did not notice my presence there above him, no one on his ship did either. He did not see any danger. I can only believe that it was Lord Aron and his mind masters, with Lord Kneth aiding them, whose mind powers were shielding my presence from Doom's attention, and from the notice of his crew and the sensors of his ship. The mind masters had incredible powers, and they had been extended in their efforts by what they had learned when they had diverted the black moon from Ares. They had learned many new and interesting things from that encounter, including a way to transport my presence and image back in time *and* space—a presence and image that also had form and substance.

I found that I was able to control my presence and my image. I could make it travel, so that I could look in on what was happening down below on Earth. So my mind watched the events on Earth that were soon to come into play before me.

There I saw my own past image sitting in my friend's home, just as it had happened many months before. I saw that I was seated in a chair in his living room and we were busy talking of my life on Ares since I had last visited him. Everything was as it had been before Earth had been destroyed. My friend sat across from me listening intently to my story. Then there was a sudden disturbance. I saw a bright flashing light and what I can only describe as a small dimensional shift in time and space, a feeling of intense vertigo seized me, and then, there before my past self, once again—stood the demon prince himself. Lord Karlath Doom!

I saw the shock and fear that registered upon my face as my past self recognized our deadly intruder and I quickly got up from the chair to confront him. I also saw the fear and confusion on my friend's face. Then I saw the image of Lord Doom look at that past version of myself with a gaze of intense hatred and disdain that I remembered all too well. It was chilling.

"Who are you? What is this?" my friend shouted with anger at our intruder.

Lord Doom ignored him and simply scowled at me with grim hatred, then he looked around him at the room with utter disdain, and spoke in a harsh tone, "How utterly primitive. A barbarian world of no significance whatsoever that I can see. Totally unimportant and useless. Oh well, it is of little consequence, it shall not exist much longer. This is your doing, Jon Kirk, your home world shall be no more because of you. I promised you compete defeat and destruction once. Now that I have attained the power of the Sindalki by their demise—and with the aid of the Kin-Ty-Roo—that time has come to pass."

His threat delivered, Doom was suddenly gone in a blinding flash, the image of him on Earth instantly disappeared. I knew what that meant and what was to come soon. I was ready.

"What was that? Who was he, Jon?" my friend asked that past version of myself in astonishment and fear.

"That was him—or his projected image—Lord Karlath Doom. He is here now. I am sorry," I heard the voice of my past self tell my friend.

It was near the time for me to act.

"Sorry?" I heard my friend ask my image from the past. "Why are you sorry, Jon…?"

I never answered my friend's question. There was no time.

Instantly my attention was back upon the bridge of Lord Doom's flagship where it remained stationed in high Earth orbit. I was surprised that Doom had brought only one space battleship with him on this mission, but then again, he needed only one mighty Enemy Empire warship to do his deadly work here today. There was nothing on Earth here that could stop his action. No one down on the planet—government or military in any nation—would even know what was to come or how to stop it. It would be an utter tragedy. That tragedy would not come to pass if I could do anything to stop it.

I heard Doom give the order to his crew that would set the mighty weapons ready to fire the devastating beams that would destroy the Earth. It was an entirely helpless and unprotected world that lay below them. A lone planet without any defenses against the incredible power of Doom's mighty warship. I waited for the right moment, the last possible second. Lord Aron and Lord Kneth had impressed upon me the importance of waiting for that last possible moment before I acted when all time was in alignment. I had waited long enough.

Now it was time to act.

Before Lord Doom knew what was happening—and I thanked the shielding my friends had afforded me to protect my presence upon that ship and in this mission from him—I made my image visible and drew my sword to face the Sindalki lord standing upon the deck of his bridge. I seemingly just appeared there.

The shock upon the face of the imperious Sindalki lord was astounding, but it was a sheer joy for me to see. For once I had the drop on him. I saw confusion and then fear in his face. Lord Doom was totally taken aback by my sudden appearance. He hesitated a bare moment, trying to figure the implications of why I was there, and how I had come there. I did not allow him time to think or to act. My sword was out and ready. I raised my blade and rushed at him immediately with wild rage and intense bloodlust.

CHAPTER 2

Earth in the Balance

My sword drawn, I quickly closed with Lord Karlath Doom.

"You!" he shouted at me in furious shocked rage.

"Yes, it is I, Jon Kirk, come to upset all your evil plans once again."

"Kirk! What are you doing here? How are you here?" Doom blurted still astonished at my sudden appearance upon the bridge of his own warship.

"I am here to kill you," I stated simply.

"Kill me? Hah, you tried that once already and I just reanimated. You know that I can not die. What makes you think you have a better chance now?"

"Actually, you can die and I have killed you *twice* already," I informed him with a grimly determined frozen gaze.

"Twice?" Doom whispered, quickly thinking it over, trying to figure out the implications, as he moved away from me. I could see the fear in his face now.

"Yes, and I think this third time will be the charm. Prepare to die!"

"We shall see about that!" Doom screamed and then suddenly came at me with his own drawn sword. It was an unexpected action but I welcomed it.

Our blades clashed in mighty fury. I went back at him in a hard attack with my weapon as our swords clashed in a resounding torrent of loud clanging turmoil. Sparks flew all around us. The wide eyes of every member of his bridge crew watched us intently, but did not interfere. They were all terrified. We were deep in battle rage. We fought furiously. He was able to push me back. I would not accept defeat. Our lives and the fate of the Earth were in the balance.

I came at Lord Doom once again and hit him hard. He deflected my blade once, twice, and then a third time. I came at him still harder, faster, he was surprised by my agility—my Earthly muscles and stamina giving me an edge in battle he had never figured I possessed. Or he had forgotten about my Earthly abilities. He tried to move off to safety. I saw that he was about to escape me by using his Sindalki magic to hide himself in some nether dimension—open the door and hide—but he had only one ship here, so there was no other vessel for him to run to. It also seemed that his mind powers and super science were being somehow tamped down and had become unusable. I thought I knew the reason. I smiled a grim thanks to Lord Aron and Lord Kneth, for I saw their actions here in blocking Lord Doom's powers and his escape.

I acted quickly. Doom turned to escape me and I blocked him, as I turned to meet him. He came at me with a vicious downward cut. I knocked his sword away, and while he tried to use his mind master powers upon me one more time—I could tell that he was being blocked, Lord Aron and Lord Kneth had done their job well—Lord Doom was unable to effect my thoughts. Doom was not able to use his mental powers against me. I knew that I had him then.

I came at him hard then and he tried to turn away, to escape once again, but I cut him off and then met him face to face. His look showed terror for the first time. He was trapped and he knew it. I moved forward.

"Your time has run out, Lord Doom." I stated with grim determination.

"I can not die!"

"We shall find out about that now!" I shouted.

I immediately plunged my blade down to the hilt into Doom's chest, deeply into his foul black heart. He shuddered, shaking and then looked at me in great surprise as if he could not believe what had just happened. Blood flowed, then he dropped down, and I looked him over carefully. His heart had definitely stopped. He was surely dead. For now.

No sooner did I withdraw my weapon than I knew what I had to do to stop him from regenerating. I next plunged my bloody blade straight down into his eye, deep into his brain, right into his very mind, where his true powers were located. I had been able to kill him this way once in my present timeline, and now in this past timeline I would do so again, for I knew that it would work. It had worked once before. It *must* work now.

It did!

Lord Doom died instantly. His body fell down dead to the cold metal floor of his ship's bridge. He was dead and gone now. Not one of the crew upon that bridge made a move or uttered a word about what I had done. They watched what had transpired astounded and fearful. There was no opposition at all from any of his ship's crew.

I looked for the captain of the flagship and called out to him, "You—come here!"

It was a Tergat, one of the tall yellow-hued finned humanoids which I now knew that both empires used as *consignat* crew and warriors—indentured military warriors would be the best way to describe them. "Come here! What is your name?"

"Taku, Captain Taku," he replied looking at me closely and, no doubt, at what I had just done, with great concern. I could see he feared for his life. That was good.

"You no longer serve Lord Doom. You now serve me, Jon Kirk, Emperor of Ares. Do you understand?"

"Yes, my—My Emperor!"

"Good, now I order you to take this ship to Ares where you will turn it and the crew over to my fleet Admiral Quarto-Zar for disposition."

"I…" Taku responded in awe, obviously confused.

"Do—you—understand, Captain Taku?" I demanded in a booming voice that brooked no opposition.

The captain looked carefully upon the dead carcass of Lord Doom. He saw no indication of impending regeneration. Finally he looked into my own fiery eyes and bowed and told me, "Yes, My Emperor, it shall be done just as you say."

"Good, and know that I will be watching you, Captain," I warned the nervous Tergat, as I added, "Dispose of Lord Doom's body out your airlock and see to it that it is sent on a course that will take it into the nearby sun where it will burn into fiery destruction."

"It shall be done at once!" the captain replied dutifully.

"See to it now," I ordered him.

Then my presence and image began to disappear from his ship's bridge.

In a flash of sudden light—*I was gone*.

* * * *

I awoke back upon Ares, back in Tarcos, back in my own present timeline, with Lord Aron and Lord Kneth standing around me curiously. Ras-noor ordered the transport machine be turned off. Sirah, my beloved wife was there to hug me tightly and we kissed passionately, as she welcomed me back from the world of the past. It was the best welcome home ever.

"Were you successful?" Sahn-jor, my First Minister, asked me.

"Is your Earth saved?" Zaor, my best friend added impatiently.

"I think so. Lord Doom is certainly dead. I mean, the Lord Doom of that past timeline, is dead. I killed him just before he gave the order for Earth's destruction," I stated carefully, then nodded my head with certainty. "It is the third time I have killed that monster, let us hope he shall stay dead this time. I had his corpse sent out in space on a trajectory that would take it into old Sol, the bright yellow sun of my world, to burn itself to oblivion. I am sure he is gone forever now."

"I am sure that he is, Jon Kirk," Lord Kneth told me with a sharp nod of his head.

I looked to the last remaining Sindalki, the last of his people, and just nodded to him gravely.

As I got up and out of Ras-noor's machine, Sirah came rushing into my arms and we hugged and kissed once more. With Sirah now in my arms all was well in my world once again.

I walked over to Ras-noor where he was looking into another of his super-science vision instruments that had been the legacy of the Ancients of Ares. It was a device from before the Winged-men had come to Ares, from a time before the Secret Empire of the Hundred World and even before the Sindalki.

"What is it, Ras-noor?" I asked concerned, for the wily old scientist was forever seeking to revive the ancient sciences, and what he was looking at now seemed to interest him very much. "What do you see?"

"Ah, Jon Kirk, nothing bad. What I see is that the new second asteroid belt in your Sol System is now gone. It has apparently just disappeared. It has been replaced by a most lovely blue world—the one that was there before Lord Doom destroyed it. Jon Kirk, you have done it, Earth is back!"

I took a long and loving look through his vision device to see the evidence for myself. There was no denying that I had been success-ful. Earth was back. I looked at the image of the lovely blue world with awe and a feeling of intense joy. Billions who had died—did not die. The planet was safe. I do not know how Ras-noor's vision device worked, or how it allowed us to see so far through space, so clearly. It was the work of the long ago Ares ancients, bless them, but there was my home world of the Earth, now safe. I could see that it was right where it belonged, between Mars and Venus. I could see it plainly. The Earth, and its moon, were back— so all that had been done, had been undone. Everything was as it had been before, and as it should be. I sighed, thanked God I had been successful in my time travel venture, and I thanked my friends for all their help.

"My heart is truly healed now!" I stated with a wide joyful grin.

Time travel. We had done it! I had done it! Lord Aron and his people had done it really. It seemed inconceivable. But it was true. This meant some interesting possibilities that were not lost upon me for future ventures.

Of course my friend, Zaor, being a general and a fighting man was the first to broach me upon this topic, "Jon Kirk, this may be something we might be able to use as a weapon. If so, it could prove devastating."

I nodded, that was certainly true and I thought it over carefully before I replied. "Powerful certainly, but it can be very dangerous. If we ever use it again it must be used with care and serious thought to unintended consequences. It is not something to make use of lightly. One wrong move and we could create unimagined chaos."

Zaor nodded, he understood the implications of such mighty power.

Aron The Eldest wisely advised us, "The empire of time is best left alone, not to be tampered with."

Lord Kneth added heavily, "Even we Sindalki were fearful of the use of time travel because of the complicated consequences. We never did employ it as a weapon, but we understood the concept and we knew how it might be accomplished. Before the advent of the Enemy Empire we did not overly consider it, since we reigned supreme in the Known Universe. We did not want to introduce the attendant temporal contradictions and dangers into our calculations. One wrong move and a person—or an entire planet—could blink out of existence."

I listened to their warnings and advice and realized they were right. Having such a powerful weapon and *using* it however were two different things entirely. I was somewhat aware of the theories and principles. I had read enough paperback science fiction when I was a youngster growing up on Earth before I went to fight in Vietnam. These were incredible time travel stories in the SF mags of the day, also I recalled Ace paperback novels by Philip K. Dick and H. Beam Piper, along with Ballantine editions by Robert Silverberg and other great writers. All dealt with the implications of time travel. So I knew the very real dangers that could creep in and cause devastating time travel complications.

"I will take serious heed of all your sage advice upon this matter, my friends," I told them seriously. "Though this is a matter that might be best taken up at some other time. For now I am just happy that Earth is back where it belongs and that the billions who should never have died, have not died. We have defeated Lord Doom's plan and reversed his destruction. We have killed Lord Doom. That is a good thing, is it not?"

"It is a good thing, my husband," Sirah told me with a warm kiss.

CHAPTER 3

What Next?

I took it upon myself to allow a small celebration of our victory for the people of Ares. It was celebrated also by many friends, ministers, advisors and various military leaders of the empire I now ruled, as well as the people of all the cities on Ares. It seemed that we all deserved a break and it helped bolster our spirits. We had all been through a lot of turmoil lately. A lot had changed. Now that Earth had been saved and was once again safe I was much very relieved. I was happy about that of course. Lord Karlath Doom was certainly—most absolutely and eternally—dead. He was dead for sure this time. I allowed a deep breath of relief over that turn of events as well. That monster was gone forever. His danger posed against Sirah, myself and Ares was at an end. Then there was the major fact that the black moon had been diverted safely away from Ares, so that my new world, and all of us here were safe too.

At least for now.

But I knew a far greater threat loomed ahead.

The alien entity called the Kin-Ty-Roo.

What to do about that?

For now, Lord Doom's fleet of warships was under the command of Admiral Quarto-Zar. All officers and crew having come over to our side had sworn allegiance to the new empire I now ruled—and to myself, Jon Kirk, as Emperor of the Greens, of Ares and all planets of the Known Universe. I know, it was a bit much, certainly a mouthful for any title, but while I did not take it all that seriously I allowed it because it cemented the bonds of our people together under one leader. I knew that was important. The fact that I was that leader, did not impress me at all, but while it was an honor and duty I had never sought—nor did I enjoy—in truth I knew I was the only one who could hold together and unite all the diverse parts of this most diverse empire. Should I ever step down from my duty as ruler of the empire, that empire would devolve into civil war and a mass of squabbling worlds with disastrous violent results. Warlords would rule various worlds and then battle among themselves. I was well aware of this fact from human history so I knew my duty. I would do my duty. I really had no choice.

This moment in time was a relatively calm period for us. At this point in time, everything seemed to be going well among the worlds I now ruled. I had—*we* had—come through terrible battles and much travail and had been victorious. With Lord Doom dead, I could breathe easier now, and not constantly fear for the life and safety of Sirah, and my small son, Alun. And with Tob and Vakon dead now, killed by Crooch—who had somehow changed his ways—still most mysterious to me—we all felt more safe and secure that these two treacherous enemies were to be feared no longer either.

Meanwhile Crooch had come back to Tarcos with me and he remained a mystery to my thoughts. I could not figure him out. He was a complex man. His sudden change in attitude and loyalty—if he even knew the meaning of the word loyalty—and I doubted it—seemed most unusual. Or perhaps his change of mind was not so unusual? I could not be sure. His sudden change, based on his utter terror of the entity, the Kin-Ty-Roo was something that I could perhaps understand, but it was still a constant surprise to me. Crooch's change of side, and his aid to me in my battle with Lord Doom, had also surprised Sirah, Zaor, Sahn-jor and many others of my inner circle who did not trust him. And with good reason. Some cautioned me about him, others pressed for me to have him executed immediately. They wanted him dead. They told me they only gave me this advice for my own protection. I thanked them, for I knew their hearts were in the right place, but I could not do it. I felt I owed Crooch something for the help he had given me. He had risked his life, after all. It was a brave action that he had taken. I could not forget it. His action had changed everything for me. I could not desert him. I was not an ungrateful person. I could never be that way, and perhaps the man had really changed for the better? Who could say for sure? He certainly had received the shock of his life from Lord Doom and the Kin-Ty-Roo. And yet my closest advisors insisted that I have him executed immediately. They told me he was better off dead. I did not agree. We were at an impasse.

"I can not do that," I told them all most carefully during a meeting on the topic, for I knew their intentions were good. "He saved my life when I was a prisoner on Doom's ship. He set me free and by that action he made our entire victory possible."

"Yes, that may be true, but I still say he can not be trusted," Zaor told me with absolute certainty. He would not drop his request, for he hated Crooch, and with good reason.

I nodded, I realized what my advisors and friends were telling me, and perhaps they were correct, but I felt that Crooch had indeed changed. There was no doubt about that. He had acted to set me free when it was most crucial. He did not have to do that. Such action was extremely dangerous for him, had Lord Doom found out about it—or won our battle, instead of myself. Crooch's action had changed everything for me. I felt I—and all of Ares—owed him something for that. Quite a lot, in fact.

I also had it in my heart that there is a redemptive factor in all people and that it is possible for a person to always change for the better, if they truly want to do so. Perhaps Crooch had done so? He had certainly proved it to me by his actions, so I wanted to give him one last chance, but not many around me were of the same mind on this matter.

"I say execute him immediately, Jon Kirk. He has committed enough acts of treason and betrayal so that his performance of merely one good deed—however important to our cause—should not save him from punishment for all the bad that he has done before," Sahn-jor counseled me with care. I was shocked that Sahn-jor insisted I do this. A man who was the most peaceful person I had ever met was speaking in such a hard manner. It got my attention. Sahn-jor was the man who had tried to make peace with the brute Grusus, the Winged-man monster who had almost conquered the Greens and laid siege to destroy Tarcos. He was not a military man or a man of violence at all. He saw the good in everyone. Yet even a peaceful man such as Sahn-jor had no use for Crooch.

"You may be right, but I can not do it," I told Sahn-jor and all the others.

"Then allow me, Jon Kirk, to do the deed," Zaor volunteered with a rather wicked little smile. He did not like Crooch at all, and I could not blame him.

"No, I will not allow it."

Zaor just shook his head at me and then stomped off in a huff showing his annoyance with what he told me were my much too charitable Earther outworlder ways.

Sahn-jor looked at me sadly, "I know you will do as you must do, Jon Kirk. Let us hope you never regret this great generosity that you bestow upon him."

"I pray that I do not," I replied, and said a silent prayer.

I looked to Sirah. She was also there at the meeting and had heard all that was said. She just gave me a wan smile, "He set you free, and that saved your life, my husband, and that act brought you back to me. I can not damn him after he did that—even though all his other actions certainly deserve death. His life is in your hands, my husband. You must make the decision."

I nodded, she was correct. I was the one to decide. I had decided. I could not do it. Honor dictated it. I owed the fellow, and so I would put all that had happened between us now in the past. Would that prove to be a great mistake—or perhaps—a most wise and just action that would yield good results? Who could say? And with a man like Crooch, who could ever know for certain.

I allowed Crooch free reign in the city and throughout the palace and gave him a position as one of my close advisors. I recognized that the devious little scoundrel certainly had a most able and nimble mind—if somewhat warped—so I was interested in what he had to say on various matters, though wary of any advice he gave me. I wanted to keep him close for another reason, so I could keep my eye on him. I knew his words could be sheer poison, and yet, he seemed to be a changed man now. This action fell in with my heartfelt belief that a man could change and become a better person if he wanted to do so. I was a man who believed in second chances. Hadn't my advent here on Ares been a second chance for me? A most wonderful second chance! In the meantime, I listened to Crooch's advice and it seemed sound, and it was not anything unusual. That became most perplexing as he had not seemed to have fallen back into his old dark ways at all, so in that way Crooch had become even more mysterious to me and to many of my advisors and ministers.

Crooch told me he very much appreciated my good treatment of him, and was most grateful for the stay of his execution, and he vowed to serve me truthfully and faithfully until he would die. I thanked him, but thought this was a bit much, though he seemed true in his feelings. Truthfulness and faithfulness—I wondered if he even knew the definition of those two words, but I did not press him upon the matter. I accepted Crooch as he was, and he in spite of all his past actions, proved to have a good mind, one that was agile and bold, and it turned out that he served me and Ares well. I was pleased with his service. However, there was one thing that stuck in my craw about him, for his advice was adamant and firm upon only one single but constant topic. It was a topic that he obsessed upon to the exclusion of all other thoughts.

"Jon Kirk, you must find a way to destroy the Kin-Ty-Roo."

"I know that Crooch," I admitted to him upon more than one occasion. I was even in agreement with him upon this matter, but it was an action much easier said than done.

"No, I fear you do not fully understand what we are dealing with here, My Emperor. The Kin-Ty-Roo is an enemy a hundred times more deadly and dangerous than even Lord Doom. It must be destroyed immediately. You must use the fleet of your vast empire, all your many space warships, all your resources such as the science of Ras-noor, and Lord Aron's mind masters. They must unite and find some way to destroy the entity soon," he told me, even pleading at times, then later almost demanding, and I could see some of the old Crooch there showing through now in the impatience of his new personality, "for we do not have much time."

"I shall do so when I make the decision, but why are you so adamant on its immediate destruction?"

"I have seen it, Jon Kirk. I have felt it inside me. I know what it wants," Crooch said, and I could see the terror in his eyes. We had spoken of this before somewhat, but now my ministers, advisors and I listened more intently as I questioned him about the alien entity and what he knew of it. He seemed to have more knowledge of the thing than I had at first anticipated. My curiosity was peaked, as was the interest of all my ministers and advisors.

"So what exactly does it want?" I asked Crooch in a firm tone. I already knew something of what this entity was about, but not in much detail. For instance, none of us knew anything about its goal or aims. Or if it even had any goals or aims. Nor anything of its origin.

"You know. Doom himself told you, Jon Kirk. It seeks to do only one thing—to simply devour. Beyond that I do not know what the thing wants, but we know that it exists to feed. That should be enough."

"Yes," I said softly in agreement with him. It was certainly enough for me.

"To feed?" Zaor asked fearfully. "How does it accomplish this? What does that really mean?"

"It is not to eat, as we do. It feeds, but massively. That means it can absorb a whole being, or an entire race, and even planets. Entire worlds. It is huge and voracious in appetite," Crooch told us with a sureness that surprised us all and a tone of utter terror that took control of his features and shone through his eyes with wild fear.

"How do you know all this?" I asked him carefully. "What makes you so sure?"

Crooch looked at me now most closely, gave a wily sneer, "When I was my old self, being in the service of Lord Doom, I listened in on his private comm while he communicated with the thing."

"You—what?" I asked astounded, the old Crooch at his best no doubt. "I thought you knew nothing of the being. You asked me about it on Doom's ship, remember?"

"Yes, I remember, but I wanted verification on what I knew, from you," Crooch told me.

"Why from me?" I asked curiously.

Crooch remained silent on this point and I wondered what he was hiding.

"Answer my question!" I demanded.

"You are essential to the plan, that is all I know, and all I can say, My Emperor," Crooch whispered softly, his eyes pleading with me.

I tamped down my anger. Was this some new betrayal? I looked at Crooch and decided we needed to get to the bottom of this.

"How were you able to do this? To listen in," Aron The Eldest suddenly spoke up in alarm, knowing this was all done through mind powers and not normal communications. Mind powers the wily Crooch did not possess.

"Yes, how indeed?" Crooch said with a wily grin. "It was of course all done by mind link, tight secure mind link, but I was able to find a device Lord Doom possessed that would allow me to listen in, and I did. My Lords, I tell you true now, the things I heard, the abominations—the terrible visions I saw—I am not at all well after it…"

Crooch looked downward, silent. There was no deviousness there now in him. Only silent terror. I almost felt sorry for him.

"And that made you decide to free me on Doom's ship?" I asked him carefully.

"Yes, Jon Kirk. I may be many things and I have done some terrible deeds in my life, but what I saw and heard that day make me wish I could take it all out of my mind and forget it for all time," Crooch told us in all sincerity, and I believed him—and I think everyone else there did as well.

Lord Aron came forward and approached Crooch, "Will you allow me and the Council of Keven Elders to enter your mind to see this for ourselves?"

I looked at Lord Aron with an inquisitive expression. Did he know something that I did not about Crooch? What was he aiming at?

"Have a care, My Lord," Crooch warned the mind master. "I have seen and heard such things…"

"I believe you," Aron The Eldest smiled with a gentleness I had not often seen from him before. "We shall be careful, believe me. We understand what is involved."

"Then yes, I will allow it," Crooch stated with a nod of his head.

"Good, then let us get ready," Lord Aron told his people as they gathered around him.

I looked at Aron in surprise, "You mean you want to do it right now, right here?"

"Of course. Why not? Now is the best time," Lord Aron stated simply and with that, his people stood in a circle and had Crooch lay down within it. Lord Kneth joined the Kevens in the circle.

"Create the mind meld," Lord Aron ordered his people.

Meanwhile Sirah and I, with Zaor and Sahn-jor, Ras-noor and Tor-nul stood by and watched in amazement at what was to transpire.

CHAPTER 4

The Kin-Ty-Roo

Lord Kneth spoke up firmly, "It is an entity, a being, a creature of some demonic kind that is most alien to this galaxy—alien to our own galaxy. It may even be derived from some other universe altogether. Who can be certain? It is known by many names; the Kin-Ty-Roo, or He or It Who Is Not To Be Named. It is the leader or power behind what we call the Enemy Empire, or the Second Empire, or the New Empire. Fleets of the two empires—theirs, and my former one—met hundreds of years ago and a great battle was fought. The Sindalki Secret Empire—who had more warships on their mission at that time—had won that battle, and in winning the battle thought they had won the war. They had not. They did not discover any other Enemy Empire ships to oppose them at that time so their supposition seemed founded on solid ground—that they had destroyed all enemy warships. At least they thought this to be true, at the time. So they thought they had destroyed all the enemy warships and the threat had been neutralized. At the time our Sindalki mind masters could not breach the enemy shields, nor discover any of their powers or where they had come from. In truth, the Sindalki had defeated only a small lightly armed survey mission—a mission sent into our galaxy from somewhere 'outside' by the Kin-Ty-Roo to discover what was available here for it to take—for it to feed upon and absorb. The entity had a plan to invade our area of The Known Universe here, and when it did, it absorbed all that vast dead corner we now call The Empty Quarter."

"That is all true," Crooch said this with a raspy halting voice. He sounded most strange, as if it did not seem to be words that were coming from his voice at all. It was very perplexing to hear his story dragged from the depths of his mind, but we all listened to what he had to say most carefully.

Crooch's words and thoughts were often jumbled within his twisted pit of a mind, they could be a bit incoherent, and he surely had a devious and poisonous festering mind after all—but the gist of what he had seen and heard during Lord Doom's report to his master those many weeks ago had shocked even him to the depths of his very being. Fear of the alien thing ran rampant within Crooch's mind, especially in the darkest corners where even he did not realize what lurked there deep within. Lord Kneth, along with Lord Aron and his Kevens probed his mind and dug it all out. Crooch was not one who had any loving or compassionate sensibilities, and it seemed that his recent change of heart had all been the result of sheer terror, survival and self-serving intentions.

"Stop! Stop the meld now!" I heard Lord Aron order in a loud shout, intense and using his voice verbally, his tone full of fear. He never shouted.

"What is it?" I asked showing the alarm in my voice.

"I—I—I—I…" Lord Aron mumbled incoherently. "Stop it!"

I ran over to him and slapped his face hard. Once, twice, yet again, "Come out of it! Aron! Break the contact! You must break the contact!"

Lord Aron suddenly collapsed in my arms. The other members of the mind meld circle shook themselves as if coming out of a bad dream. Only Lord Kneth stood up, came over to me confidently and said, "Jon Kirk, this Kin-Ty-Roo is coming for us all. I have seen it. It sees our presence of mind. We must find it and kill it before it can perform its mission."

"Mission?"

"Yes," he replied rather casually.

"You are telling me it has a mission? I thought it was just some mindless feeding thing," I asked curiously, for it seemed to me that this had been a strange word for the Sindalki lord to use.

Mission? I assumed we were dealing with a ravenous beast with an insatiable hunger for food, or a creature seeking to absorb some type of space-born matter and energy, but this seemed far more than that. If the entity truly had a mission, then what did that mean? I looked over to Lord Aron, he was regaining consciousness now. He gave me a wan grin, then shook his head as if to clear his thoughts.

"Thank you, Jon Kirk, I am better now," he told me a bit shyly, embarrassed by his lapse of control. Totally unexpected and dangerous.

"You had me—all of us—worried there for a moment, Aron," I told my friend. King Shamar now came over and also helped the Keven mind master to get to his feet.

While the king did this, I looked back at Lord Kneth, asking, "You said something before that got my attention. Something about the entity being on some…mission?"

"I think I can answer that, Jon Kirk," Lord Aron told me now obviously recovered from whatever had troubled him. "From what I saw inside Crooch's darkest memories of the event of his brief personal contact with the entity—memories even he does not remember, thank the gods—the enemy entity simply seeks to absorb everything that there is in existence."

No one said a word for a long moment about that.

"Everything?" I asked slowly, showing my open astonishment.

"Yes, everything…" Lord Aron repeated simply.

"*Everything*…like, everything in existence?" I spoke softly quite perplexed by this news, astonished by the information. What did it really mean? I asked Lord Aron and Lord Kneth to explain, "You mean people, maybe even an entire warship? Is any of that even possible?"

"Far more than that, Jon Kirk. Entire planets, and more than that even, for you see everything means *everything* I am afraid. That means the entirety of The Known Universe, gravity, mass, energy, and even the kingdom of time. All that is within the bounds of our galaxy certainly and perhaps eventually, all matter and energy that makes up other galaxies and eventually, the universe itself." Lord Aron stated firmly. The Keven was deadly serious and the stress and strain showed in his gentle face to show a stark deep sadness.

I looked at Lord Aron aghast. I could not accept what he was telling me. It was just too inconceivable. The world-wrecking consequences far too dire to even imagine. I saw Crooch nod to me fearfully in agreement with what Lord Aron had told us. Lord Kneth did likewise. All the Keven mind masters looked on in shocked reaction but all were in agreement with Lord Aron's words as well. I began to grow very fearful of exactly what we were up against here. It seemed incredible—and impossible.

"*Everything?*" I whispered numbly, dumbfounded. How could I—or anyone even —fight such an all-powerful creature—much less defeat it!

"*Everything*, certainly," Lord Aron repeated to me in a firm but sad tone that had the ring of defeat eating away at it.

I said no more. I did not know what more there was that I could say. The extent of the danger was inconceivable for a mere mortal like myself to even contemplate. What to do? I did not know. I had no idea, but I knew two things. I knew my people were looking for me to lead them and to come up with some plan that worked—and I knew I had to do something about it—very, very quickly!

CHAPTER 5

Battle Plan

Of course what I needed was a plan—and I needed a damn good one! Which was easier said than done. I needed to find a way to defeat this mysterious enemy alien entity. Before I did that however, I needed to locate it and then discover a way to get at it safely so that I could destroy it. Then, how do I destroy it?

I told all these thoughts to the members of the empire War Council the next day. I had the full council in that meeting, all the leaders of the empire that I now ruled were in attendance. Not only was there Zaor, Sahn-jor, Aron The Eldest and King Shamar, with Lord Kneth attending; but there was Winged-man Admiral Quarto of Zar; Rasnoor my science chief, and others of my ministers, advisors, and high lords. The leaders of most of the worlds throughout the empire came to the meeting as well, or appeared via image projection from their home worlds.

Thus, I was happy to see again some old friends from previous battles; the huge Viking-like Gorm of the Gorms had come in person, in all his wild fury and bluster; while projections showed up of wily Bran from the pirate world of Ko-Ah-Leh; Poln, the female felina from Caxtar; Sharn, the leader of the Tergats who stood tall and bold, his yellow-hued skin and fins making him a most strange-looking alien friend; Sasheen, the green merman from the water world of Talu, shown laying comfortably in a pool of blue Talu liquid; and even grim General Zod, commander of the Blue Korta mercenary troopers. They were all there, along with many others to communicate and learn, and to think and plan.

I began by welcoming them all and then getting down to the point of the War Council. For we were at war again now, no doubt about it.

"We have but one mission here today, my friends. We need to find a way to locate this enemy entity, the Kin-Ty-Roo, and then find a way to destroy it," I put the pressing question to the hundreds of attendees looking from face to face at most of them with a grim stern gaze. They were attentive, curious, but deeply concerned. They had a right to be.

Sirah, my wife and empress, sat besides me, and looked into my eyes hiding her growing fear. I could well imagine what she was thinking. One more battle and one more parting—and this time it might end in defeat and…perhaps it might be final. I feared that this time the result of my actions might not be one of victory. Doubt was pressing heavily in upon me. Was I pressing my luck in accepting this newest challenge? Sirah and I had been through so much together that I worried that I might just lose her this time. Perhaps my luck had run out? I prayed that was not the case and that I would be victorious one more time. Yet I had serious doubts, for I was going up against an alien thing the likes of which no man had ever fought before. Even the evil of the Sindalki lord, Karlath Doom paled into insignificance when dealing with this all-powerful and incomprehensible alien entity. And yet, I still lived—we all still lived—and with that warrior mantra ringing in my mind I knew there was always hope. And with hope can always come victory.

"Jon Kirk," my wife whispered squeezing my hand tightly. "I know you. I know you will find a way."

"If there is a way to be found, my love, but I am not so sure," I told her frankly in a soft reply for I felt a keen discouragement by what I was up against this time. Then I added, "Look out for little Alun, if I do not…you know…return."

"I will, my love," she replied firmly, then she gave me a broad smile that melted my heart, "but you will come back to me—to us—I know you only too well, my love—and you shall be victorious!"

I looked back at her with a wan smile, not trying to alarm her, drinking in the warm love of her deep confidence—a confidence that I did not feel, but that did buoy my spirits.

The War Council went on for many hours. Each speaker offering their comments and advice one after the other. Some of what they proposed was good, most of it was off the mark. I let them all speak their minds. I knew it was important for them all to state their views in their own way upon this most critical subject, however true or false they might be. These were my people now—every one of them.

I listened most carefully to speaker after speaker. Wise men who spoke in anxious tones, fighters whose voices ran with wild warrior bluster, all of it mixed with anger, fear, and other emotions overseen by worry or growing terror.

Some representatives offered what they believed might work as some form of peace deal, or they asked if some accommodation should be made with the entity. Only one time did Aron the Eldest need to give them a good visual dose, through mental mind imagery, of exactly what we had all seen in Crooch's mind—then those thoughts evaporated from everyone's mind. Soon there was no more opposition to the war. In fact, there was now avid support of it. The enemy entity had to be destroyed and that was that. But how to do it? And what was the location of the thing? We could not find it. Was it in hiding? If so, why? It seemed to have disappeared, and that seemed a very bad sign.

Crooch was at the meeting as well. Being one of my advisors, I wanted him to be there. I wanted to hear his views on the subject. As yet he had been silent. He was often very quiet. I assumed that he had what he wanted most now, for he saw that the operation he had advocated for so long was beginning to take shape. The war against the enemy entity, the Kin-Ty-Roo, was being discussed and planned. He listened quietly, patiently, but most attentively. He was eager to see action begun. There were many there who shared his view. Myself among them.

I listened closely to all that was being said by all at the War Council, and I should say that while there was a lot of discussions among all present, there was very little factual planning that came out of it. I knew the problem. A lack of facts. We were in need of detailed information before any real decision could be made for battle, and I had the creepy feeling that I was in way over my head on dealing with this problem.

Gorm, the giant stood up tall and proud. The huge fellow often reminded me of some ancient Earth Viking warrior. He held high his massive battle ax in his ham-like hands. I had been with him on boarding parties going into Enemy Empire warships, and he had used that weapon with devastating consequences. He stood up tall and said simply, "We should find their ships, wherever they are, board them, and then smash all there who oppose us!"

Gorm then smiled broadly as many their applauded him.

It was all so simple for him. I envied him.

There was then a growing chant of support for his plan—as it was. Loud cheers.

I thanked Gorm for his heartfelt words of encouragement. He gave me a wide grin that showed me he was ready to fight—that he was even anticipating it! There were many there with the same feeling, but without the proper information on how to defeat the entity— I felt we were at a dead end. I would never send any of our brave warriors out on some stupid attack that would place them in danger without the possibility of true victory. Right now, we were not in any position to instigate offensive action against the entity with any hope of success.

Sahn-jor looked over at me and allowed a tiny smile, just shaking his head showing sad frustration at Gorm's wonderful bluster, but evident lack of serious planning. He and I liked the big fellow, but Gorm was not any master strategist or tactician. He was a very direct action oriented fighter, which is what I liked so much about him. And yet, he was who he was, and he was not ashamed of the fact—nor was I ashamed of anything about him. He was Gorm of the Gorms, and it was as simple as that. In his world all problems were solved simply by force. I wished this problem could be so easily settled.

Zaor stood up out of his seat now and looked over everyone throughout the chamber most carefully. He was now the First General of the army of the empire, and he was also the first friend I had made since my arrival on Ares years ago. He spoke in a forceful tone, "I fear the army in this situation may be useless to you, My Emperor. This seems more a matter for the super-science of the Ancients of Ares, or the mental powers of the mind masters of Kev. The army and all your warriors stand ready to fight, and your Black Dragons, your imperial bodyguard chaff at the bit to follow whatever order you give them. However, even I can see that the Physical Realm can not prevail for us now. If we ever have a situation where overwhelming physical force is needed, you can count on us, but I fear this is not it, My Emperor. But knowing of the three Modes of Power: physical, super-science, and the power of the mind masters, it seems that it is wisest for the leaders in those other two areas to put forward their plans here today."

Zaor looked knowingly towards Lord Aron and Ras-noor and then sat down. He had said his piece as a warrior and fighting man. It was true advice and it was what was needed to be said. There was nothing else for him to do now. There were murmurs of approval by many there at his words, and growing anticipation to hear from the leaders who were experts in the other two areas of power.

Ras-noor, my science chief stood up then, looked around the room at all the expectant faces, nodded and began, "So be it. My teams of scientists have gone through all the machines and devices of the Ancients of Ares, we have read through *The Book of Kor* and other tomes of long lost knowledge. We have used mysterious devices to seek out this entity. We can not discern its exact location. However, we do know this, it is somewhere deep within the expansive void of space we now call The Empty Quarter."

"The Empty Quarter," I spoke the dread words softly to myself. That was bad news. I knew only fleeting information about that far away sector of deep space but it had been reported to us that bad things had happened there of late.

I looked to Ras-noor, this information was most disconcerting and I could feel his disappointment that he could not add more to his words as he silently sat back down in his seat. I was much disappointed at this news.

Kal-at, one of his talented scientific associates, then spoke up to explain to us all, "The Empty Quarter is now a vast area of our Known Universe in which the entity had recently been feeding when it had invaded the space of the former Secret Empire of the Sindalki. The entity, and its massive fleet held complete control of this area of space from the Sindalki—now we have lost all contact with the worlds located there. It is now a vast empty blackness. Suns, planets, everything seem to be gone. Gone, and we can not discover where any of these worlds and suns have gone to. It is inexplicable. We can not contact them, nor see any evidence of their existence. We can not imagine such a mystery and while we wondered just what had happened—and have many theories upon what it might mean—we are not sure at all what has gone on in that dark area of space. It is an empty void closed off to our warships and to our detection devices. The mind masters were also effectively blocked from learning what has happened there. We fear utter destruction of all the suns, planets and civilizations that had once flourished there. It is a terrible thing to even consider."

Kal-at then sat down. He had issued his report and it was grim.

Aron The Eldest now took to his feet to address the attendees to make his own report. "We of Kev, with the assistance of the Sindalki, Lord Kenth, have not been able to create a mind meld powerful enough to search the many planets and star systems of our part of the Known Universe for this entity. The distances are just too vast for us to deal with now. However, there is a theory that Lord Kneth has put forth to me and I am looking into that now. It may increase our scanning range substantially."

"What may that be, my friend?" I asked quickly, grasping at this straw he offered that might help us.

"There is said to be an ultimate force of power, known as the Sacred Ku, which is normally closed off to us, and it is generally unattainable. However, the Sacred Ku may hold the answer we need to produce greater power and range in our mind meld, far greater range and distance."

"How does this work?" I asked intrigued now, allowing some hope to enter my thoughts and the tone of my voice which others there picked up upon.

"It is most complicated, My Emperor," Lord Aron told me respectfully. "The Sacred Ku is some kind of amalgamation of the minds of all the dead Ancients of Ares since the beginning of time. The minds of other beings are also involved. In fact, it seems endless in content."

"It is endless, and do not forget the Sindalki," Lord Kneth offered quickly. "The Sindalki minds of all our dead are also included in the Sacred Ku, as well as all other races from so many worlds it is inconceivable. Too many worlds even to mention."

Lord Aron nodded, "Very true, My Lord Kneth. This multitude of minds are still somewhat active even though their physical bodies may have died millennia ago. We know there is some remnant of the former living tissue—the energy spirit of the mind if you will, that still exists. It exists somewhere in the regions of nether space. While their bodies have died normal death over millennia, there is still some shadow of all their minds that still lives on."

"Are you talking about the soul?" I asked, astonished by this seeming evidence of the human and Earthly theory of some form of life after death, spoken to me by a man of Ares.

"We know not of this Earthly term, My Emperor, but perhaps it is the same thing. I know not for certain," Lord Aron replied humbly.

"I see. So tell me, what do you plan to do?"

"We plan to use the Sacred Ku, to make contact with it and use it to expand the power and reach of our mind meld to locate this Kin-Ty-Roo and destroy it. If possible."

"And I can aid them in this too, Jon Kirk," Ras-noor added proudly. "The super-science of the Ancients of Ares made possible brain wave augmentation devices of vast power. Recently we took many of the smaller devices and connected them to form a more powerful energy stream. These devices empower and expand the powers of the mind. My teams are working on even newer devices now, far larger ones, very powerful, and these may aid Lord Aron and his mind masters substantially in contacting the Sacred Ku."

I nodded approval. It seemed like a plan to me. I myself did not have anything to offer to it, for these super science and mystical mind powers were far beyond my simple warrior understanding, but I gave the order to move on it as quickly as possible.

"How soon can we be in operation? Time is limited. The entity is coming for us—and I had rather we went to *it* to do battle, before *it* gets here. I do not want to wait until it comes here to Ares to wreak destruction. Also, the other planets of the empire must be protected, and I do not want them to become defenseless targets. We must save all our worlds. With that in mind, Ras-noor, how are things progressing on the new platform ray projectors?"

"Very well, Jon Kirk, very well. My team has already built larger and more powerful ray projectors and set them upon the mountains of both continents of Ares, as well as in orbit around the planet. Ares is well protected now, I believe. We have also transported hundreds of these defense platforms to many of the worlds throughout the empire: Gorm, Ko-Ah-Leh, Caxtar, Tergat, Talu, Korta and even Zar."

"That is good to hear and I know the leaders and people of all those worlds will feel some relief at hearing that. We will do all we can to protect all our worlds. Now I need to know how soon we can set our plan against the entity in motion?" I asked impatiently.

Aron The Eldest spoke up then, "We are doing so now, Jon Kirk. As you often say, the wheels are set in motion. We will make contact with the Sacred Ku soon and through it—if possible—find the location of the alien entity. However, once we contact the Sacred Ku, there could be a problem."

I shook my head in frustration. "What now? Continue Lord Aron, please explain. What problem?"

"Jon Kirk, the entity once found must be dealt with. That may mean many things, for there are many ways to deal with such a powerful creature—sheer destruction may not suffice. The old books tell us that there is one sure way that this can be accomplished. It requires the sacrifice of our most heroic and powerful warrior to confront it in a physical confrontation—what would be a momentous and epic battle."

"But how so? What kind of battle?"

"A physical *personal* battle, My Lord."

"You mean one on one—a personal battle with weapons, with … what, swords?"

"Swords, or ray guns, projectile weapons, it matters not the weapon, so long as the physical personal aspect is present in the battle. It might even be done through the use of a fleet of warships—but the commander of that fleet must be a single heroic man who is the supreme leader and the one personal commander completely in charge of our forces and giving the orders for all that will happen."

"I do not understand. You have super science ray weapons, vast mental powers…"

"Yes, and all shall be in use and stressed to the ultimate to hold the entity powers at bay. The entity can only be held at bay for a short period of time—if that be possible at all—but we pray it may be long enough for a mighty warrior such as yourself to enter its most sacred domain—and slay it."

I looked at Lord Aron astounded by his words. Me? Why me? He wanted me to go up against the alien entity alone, to fight it to the death—to slay this terrible thing called the Kin-Ty-Roo? What was that all about? It was crazy, insane, probably even suicide! I saw Crooch shudder in terror at the very thought. He closed his eyes and turned his face away from me. I think he was crying. I was astonished and gritted my teeth, but if I must do it—then I would do what was needed to protect my family and my people.

Zaor stood up boldly, "I shall do it!"

Tor-nul, the captain of my Black Dragons, stood up beside him speaking firmly, "And I shall help him!"

"Let us not get too far ahead of ourselves here," Lord Kneth stated in his wise old voice. "There is much that needs to be done ere we ever reach that point. And there is one other matter of major importance. There can be only one man we can send to do personal battle with the entity. The man we send to battle the entity must be Jon Kirk, and Jon Kirk *only*. I am afraid there can be no other. He is an Earth man, an outworlder among us all. Only an outworlder can ever hope to defeat the Kin-Ty-Roo, for it is an outworld entity as well. Such truths are explicitly written in *The Book of Kor*, and in other even older Sindalki tomes. So the battle is set, we have our champion, now we only need to make the fight happen."

I hardly knew what to say to all this. I was shocked certainly and surprised, but if it was my duty as an Earthman to do this thing, to fight and die for my people, then I would not shirk that duty. Perhaps, as an Earthman, I would have some advantage against this entity? I did not think it possible, but wiser heads than I, including Lord Aron, Lord Kneth, and even old Ras-noor felt that this was the way to go. I patted the short sword in a scabbard hanging from the belt at my side; I felt for my trusty Colt .45 auto that I'd had with me since I had first come to Ares. I knew it was loaded and ready for action. I, however, was not, for I had great concern and trepidation about what was to come. And with good reason.

I took a deep breath, nodded my acceptance of my new duty, then said firmly, "I accept the challenge. I will do it!"

So I accepted the challenge. I would do what was required of me, whatever was asked of me. Whatever it might be. It is the duty of a warrior and a fighting man to fight for those he held dear, to protect and serve those who needed protection.

I stood up and spoke simply, "If Lord Aron and Ras-noor can locate this enemy entity—if they can find a way to get me into contact with it—then I will go there and slay the damn thing!"

There were cheers from every voice in that huge assemblage. I could see the hope growing now upon the faces of each one of them as they digested my words and allowed a renewal of hope to show from their eyes. I know that many there felt that with Jon Kirk going to fight the alien entity, then victory was now certainly assured. They even told me as much. I smiled back at them, I was honored, of course. But I was not sure about any of this at all.

CHAPTER 6

The Sacred Ku

It was two days later when Zaor called me to accompany him to a large secret chamber located in the deep dark cellars below the palace in Tarcos. This was an immense area that was not often used. It was now made into a well lit place where Lord Aron, Lord Kneth and all the Kevens were forming a secret mind meld ring. It was something the likes of which had never been done before. My chief scientist, Ras-noor and some members of his team were there as well, working on large complicated devices that I knew had been created with the super-science of the Ancients of Ares. These were mind machines of some kind. I did not entirely understand their use or function but I knew they were powerful complicated devices. And they could be dangerous.

As I entered the room I noticed that the entire area seemed to hum with the soft low trill of human voices, and they seemed to be joined by the rather soothing soft humming of the mysterious machines and devices working together in some form of symbiotic system. These scientific devices were strange to me, apparently electrical in some manner, but where they derived their power from, I did not know. I assumed it was from some sort of built-in battery and I asked Ras-noor about it.

"No, My Emperor, no battery would sustain the amount of power needed to run these great machines," he told me as he continued working on calibrating his mysterious devices. I felt a bit like a fish out of water when it came to these strange machines, but Ras-noor and his people seemed to understand them well enough.

"I see. Then where does the power come from?" I asked a bit exasperated by his curt response to my question. I understood he was busy, but...

He looked at me, nodded sagely, then smiled.

"The power comes from the very air, from all around us, from the tiniest and most miniscule of particles that make up all matter and energy, My Lord," he said simply, as if I now understood it all through his simple explanation. Of course, I did not completely understand what he meant, but it did not matter, as long as he and his people understood it that was important. I understood enough, for I knew what I needed to know.

I looked at the old green master scientist carefully, surprised once again by the depth of Ancient Ares super-science. It brought to my mind thoughts of atoms and even sub-atomic particles, and thoughts of matter transmission of some type I remember from my reading as a student back on Earth. In my youth, years before I had ever went to war or left Earth, I had been a fan of science fiction and had read a lot of those type books. I had fond memories of all those science fiction adventure stories from my youth, especially the works of Edgar Rice Burroughs and Robert E. Howard. So I had some idea of what Ras-noor might be talking about with his notions of super-science. However, none of the type of thing he was actually *doing* now had been known on Earth in practice during my time. It had all been only conjecture or theory. On Earth, even today, all of this science was just the stuff of fantastic fiction. None of this power, other than atomic energy, had even been discovered on Earth. Most of what Ras-noor was doing here now was only surmised by the most imaginative Earth writers in popular science fiction stories that were first published in so many old paperbacks I fondly remember reading from my youth. It was amazing and fascinating to me that these forces and powers actually existed and that we had access to it all here now on Ares.

I looked over at Ras-noor who was busy working on adjusting one of his massive machines. "You have done well, my friend."

He smiled back at me truly touched by my kind words to him, but too dedicated to his work to do more than respond with a quick, "Thank you, Jon Kirk. My only regret is that my work will place you in so much danger."

"That is all right, even though I know that it will be the fight of my life—for my very life," I said firmly, then I gave him a sly grin.

"No, Jon Kirk, you are wrong there, my friend—it will be a fight for *all* our lives, I am afraid," Ras-noor corrected me with a sad look in his eyes. "If you fail—then we all fail."

I nodded deeply, "I know. Well, I am grateful to do my duty and I will do it to the best of my ability."

"We know that, My Emperor, no one can ask more of you than that. Let us hope you will be successful—for we have no other road to victory other than through your battle and defeat of this alien thing."

Wily old Ras-noor really knew how to put on the pressure.

I nodded, said a curt, "Then so be it!"

* * * *

Work on the mind meld ring progressed. Each member of the ring was now in close mental contact with all others. It was explained to me that they were literally inside each others minds, building what they termed a mind platform to expand their meld far and wide. Meanwhile, Ras-noor's devices were in operation and they amplified their brain waves a hundred fold, then a thousand fold. There was a tingling of electricity or some other force we could all feel in the air throughout the huge chamber. There was the faint odor of something burning. I recognized the smell and thought that it might be… Could it be flesh? That got my attention. It was a most disconcerting odor. I grew concerned. Could it be brain matter that was burning? I hoped there was no way that could be true. I looked up horrified at the men forming the mind ring and grew concerned for their safety. They seemed to be calm enough though, there were no signs of outward distress among any of them at all. It was most strange. Lord Aron and Lord Kneth, the leaders of the mind masters, worked tirelessly to shape and form the meld and give it focus and direction.

"We have now contacted the Sacred Ku!" Lord Kneth announced suddenly. I could see the concern growing upon his face. He was not at all certain how this was going to end up.

I, along with the many spectators there who were not involved in the process: Sirah, Zaor, Sahn-jor, Gorm, and many others watched with awe and astonishment at what the mind masters were beginning to achieve.

Then it began! The room began to swirl around us. The walls and ceiling and floor seemed to have disappeared instantly. It was as if they had just dropped away. We suddenly found ourselves floating in the utter blackness of outer space. Twinkling stars and all manner of planets, blazing suns and shooting comets moved all around us. It was magical, mysterious, amazing and terrifying all at once. It was also exquisitely beautiful. I knew this was not real, it had to be some type of projection because I could still feel the solid floor of the room beneath my feet, the walls of the palace's underground cellar were still there as well—but none of it was visible to us now. Now we saw what the mind meld showed us. We, being spectators, worked to calm our initial shock and panic and stood together in a small group holding each other tightly as we watched the miraculous process taking place all around us.

I had a thousand questions for Lord Aron and Lord Kneth naturally about what was happening, about the visions we saw all around us, but they were far too busy now to be bothered by my inquisitiveness—even had I dared ask them my questions then. I just stood there with the others in our small group and watched what was going on all around us in abject amazement. It seemed almost magical, but it was not magic at all. It as a form of super science unknown upon the Earth.

"Behold, the Sacred Ku are among us now!" Lord Aron spoke up in a firm voice, but I knew he was also mind-speaking his words. "We welcome you all, mighty ancestors of all the beings of all the worlds, of all time and space, and we seek contact with you now."

There was no reply.

There would be no reply as such.

The star field around us just began to swirl and glow with a more maddening frenzy, then with a faster and very dizzying feeling that began to effect us all. However, this seemed not to effect anyone who was part of the actual inside meld ring—but it surely effected all of us who were outside of it.

We, the spectators, grew dizzy and near panic now as the field around us swirled faster and more frantic in its powerful motion. It was almost as if we could feel the anger and rage from the force that had just been contacted because of being detected and disturbed. I began to grow a bit concerned at what was happening, and I hoped this had not been a big mistake. I was not so sure now about what we were attempting. I hoped we were doing the right thing. It was all incredibly hypnotic, terrifying—then it suddenly stopped and all time and space around us went back to the normal and peaceful star field of before. We each let out a deep breathe of relief.

"We have indeed made contact," Lord Aron announced triumphantly.

There was total silence now—deadly pin-drop silence. I don't think anyone in that vast chamber even took another single breath for a full minute.

I did not know whether to cheer in joy or shout out in terror. We seemed to be delving into things here that I had never anticipated, never desired, and did not especially like dealing with. It was terrifying, strange, incomprehensible. But if it meant saving Ares from that damn alien entity and defeating it somehow, then I was all for it.

Go on, Aron, Lord Kneth, I shouted silently with the thoughts inside my mind, *Do your damnedest!*

"It is done," Lord Aron suddenly spoke up as if in answer to my thoughts. The star field disappeared and the members of the mind meld sat up, stretched their legs, and spoke softly among themselves about the wonders they had just experienced.

CHAPTER 7

The Entity

"The Kin-Ty-Roo is in a faraway location, Jon Kirk. It seems to be on a planet many light years away by space travel. It would take you many days to get there by spaceship, though only hours away by the use of our mental powers in a special meld, when augmented by Ras-noor's devices and with the aid of the Sacred Ku," Lord Aron explained to me carefully. His face showed much stress and strain and I was sure that just gaining this small amount of knowledge had cost him dearly in stress and mental energy.

"Can you place me there?" I asked carefully. "Is there some way you can transport me—I mean my physical body—with your mind powers to this place where the entity is located?"

Lord Aron and Lord Kneth looked at each other thoughtfully, quietly for a long moment.

Then Lord Kneth nodded.

"It can be done," Lord Aron told me with a short tilt of his head, but I could see the regret in his face. I knew what that meant. He felt that it might be a death sentence for me to go there—and I had the same dark feeling about it—but it was my duty as a fighting man, so that was it. It would be done on my order, if they could make it possible.

"I will go with you, Jon Kirk," Zaor added standing at my side now, his hand set reassuringly upon my shoulder.

"I, as well!" Tor-nul spoke up bravely.

I looked at my two warrior friends and was touched by their bravery and loyalty, but I knew this was a one-man job—and I was the one man—*the only man*—to see it through. Then as if reading my thoughts on the matter Lord Aron spoke up in explanation.

"No, no one else may go on this mission, there is power enough only to transport one physical body through the vast distance of space in safety at this time—power enough only to keep that one body alive and safe and to protect it when it reaches the Kin-Ty-Roo. The one we send will need all our power and attention to keep him alive. In the future, with the aid of the Sacred Ku, we may be able to expand upon the amount of people we can transport in this manner, but for now it can only be one man—and that man is you, Jon Kirk."

"That is fine with me," I stated, ready and eager to go.

Lord Aron gave me a wan smile that caused me to look at him curiously.

"Lord Aron, what do you mean when you say when I reach the Kin-Ty-Roo?" I asked curiously. "What exactly does that mean?"

"Yes, I expected your question. In truth, it is not all that clear how I can answer this, but it seems that the planet that is the location of the entity—is also called Kin-Ty-Roo," Lord Aron explained in a low tone.

"All right, so then the entity is located upon some planet, and the name of the world is also Kin-Ty-Roo? Then if the name of the planet is Kin-Ty-Roo, then you are telling me that it is also the name of the entity?" I asked nodding my head curiously, trying to get this straight and wondering exactly what he was trying to tell me. What did Lord Aron mean?

Lord Aron only looked at me with a wan gaze of what I took to be almost abject despair.

"You are making me nervous," I told him in a low voice.

"I apologize, Jon Kirk," Lord Aron replied softly.

I looked at him carefully now and asked him sharply, "So exactly what do you mean? Exactly where upon this planet is the entity located? How can I find it? How big is it? Can you transport me directly to where it is?"

"Jon Kirk, perhaps we have not made ourselves clear," Lord Kneth explained to me in a more serious tone, a dark tone that I felt might be my death knell. "I apologize, for the concept is rather astounding to us all. It has perplexed us quite a bit. The planet Kin-Ty-Roo—*the entire planet*—well, it seems that *is* the entity."

I looked back at the Sindalki lord in surprise and utter shock.

"The entire planet is the entity!"

I was dumbfounded by this news. I surely had never expected that.

"Are you certain?" Gorm of the Gorms spoke up now shaking his huge horned-helm head in utter consternation. "The entire planet is the thing?"

Lord Kenth nodded his head slowly.

"So this entire planet is the actual entity? That is incredible!" I told Lord Aron trying to get a grip on exactly what I was dealing with here. It seemed a lot more than I had ever anticipated. Being transported to the entity to fight it with a sword, or a death ray gun, was one thing—fighting an entire planet was something else altogether. It was inconceivable and seemingly impossible. How could I even do that? How could I fight and win against a planet-size thing that was a living, thinking, malevolent alien being?

"It is all one entity. The entire planet Kin-Ty-Ro *is* the Kin-Ty-Roo," Lord Aron explained carefully with a look upon his face that did not inspire me at all.

I sighed deeply and nodded accepting the situation and my duty for what I was afraid it might be—a suicide mission. Then I shook my head in utter disbelief that it had all come down to this. It was hard for me to accept and understand. It seemed impossible, crazy even. It appeared I was defeated before I even began my battle. Yet I would perform my duty and do what was expected of me to the best of my ability, even though I was very fearful of the outcome. I steeled my nerves, I would not give up! I would defeat this thing— even at the cost of my own life! However, victory over it without my death was the optimal choice, so I considered how I might attain that result now.

"There must be something I can do to defeat this thing, and maybe even live through this battle?" I asked those around me. They looked dubious, always a bad sign. "Come now, give me some way that I can have a chance, however slim, at least to slay the creature?"

It was wily Ras-noor who offered me a possible lifeline.

"There may be some controlling area within it, a heart or brain in our own term of thinking perhaps, but certainly not anything like that at all—but there could be some type of controlling system to this thing," Ras-noor put forth hopefully. "There must be."

I nodded, grasping at the words he was offering me, looking at the wiser men around me for some further answers. This made sense to me. I waited.

Lord Kneth nodded, allowed a hard grim look, "There is a place, it is called the Place of Meaning deep within the entity. We do not know exactly what it is, or its purpose, but it seems to hold some significance for the entity. So with that in mind, we see it as being important. It may be an area to investigate. More than that we cannot say."

"The Place of Meaning?" I repeated the ominous words over verbally and within my mind. What exactly did that mean?

"It is vast, Jon Kirk, deep inside the planet, deep inside the entity of the Kin-Ty-Roo. It is there where you must be placed if you are to do battle with it."

"So then that is the target location. That is the area inside the thing where I must go to do battle against it?" I asked carefully, wanting to know for sure what they planned for me. I also asked about the creature itself. The physical appearance—but they could not help me with any of that. They told me it was all blocked to their viewing. The entity was apparently some kind of voracious monster absorbing worlds and masses of matter and energy with incredible tenacity — but now suddenly it had stopped its absorption of all matter and energy. It had suddenly ceased its feeding. It was inconceivable that it could do this massive absorption at all. What was even more strange is that it had apparently now stopped feeding altogether. Why?

When I asked those around me how the entity accomplished its feeding, Ras-noor put forward the possibility that the being was in some way made up of—or encompassed—a vast gravity well of unthinkable power. This gravity well literally sucked in and absorbed all matter and energy that came within its path—then it compacted it all through the unimaginable intensity of super massive gravity into tiny areas of intense pressure and even greater forces of still more intense gravity.

I looked at Ras-noor's explanation in shocked surprise, but then thought of all those science fiction stories I had read as a youngster back on Earth. They had seemed to touch upon this subject in some way, at least in theory. I realized now that Ras-noor seemed to be describing some kind of hyperspace tube, or perhaps even a black hole—but one that was itself a being that contained a high form of malevolent intelligence. The very idea was incredible and, I realized, extremely terrifying. How in all reason could I even fight such a monster? But fight it I must!

"So then this Place of Meaning is where I must be sent? That is my target?"

"There is no other area that we can see worthwhile to send you, Jon Kirk," Lord Kneth told me as though that was all there was to it. It was so simple for him.

I shrugged, "So be it. When do I leave? Let us get this over quickly as I have much important work to do, and little time to do it," I said boldly allowing as much bluster as I could manage in my bold words to hide my fear and dread at what I must do.

For in truth, I was utterly terrified by what I was about to attempt, and I had absolutely no idea on how I was to accomplish this mission—or if victory was even possible. In fact, I was pretty sure that victory might be impossible. I was terrified, but tried not to show it. This was because I was sure that I would never see Sirah, Alun, or Ares ever again, and this caused me great distress. I feared I would never see them again. My lovely wife and young son. I was so sure of this. My heart broke at the very thought but I had a job to do, a duty to perform. Even though I was now a powerful man, an emperor even, I was first of all a soldier with a mission, and I would not shirk my duty and that mission to disappoint those who relied upon me. I was also sure that what I was about to embark upon was most probably a fool's errand. I was fearful and anxious but ready to go, for I had a duty that I could not neglect. People depended on me and I would not let them down. I would do all I could to grasp victory. I was a warrior, a fighting man, a sergeant in the United States Army, and a proud American, so I would do what I must to bring us victory.

"All right then, let us get started," I ordered briskly, impatient.

Ras-noor spoke up and gave his people an order, the mind machines were turned on and in a short time they were all operational. They were soon humming away in a soothing machine-type of speech. Their sound was comforting in a way, almost hypnotic. I wondered if it was intended to be so.

"Form the mind meld my brothers," Aron The Eldest spoke up and his group of Kevens, with Lord Kneth, now all joined to form a circle. "Jon Kirk, please step into the center of the ring."

I hugged Sirah tightly, kissed her fiercely and said a fond good-bye as I left her to walk towards the mind meld circle.

"Come back to me, my Jon Kirk," Sirah whispered softly, bravely holding back her tears.

"I will—at least I will try to do so, my love," I answered softly, then I took a deep breath and entered the circle.

"The meld is complete, now build it larger, increase the power and range," Lord Aron ordered, and then moments later, "Now seek contact with the Sacred Ku and pray that it responds to our request for help. For without their aid we are lost."

It was unknown if this ancient universal force would even answer Lord Aron's plea for help this time. The Sacred Ku was a most enigmatic universal force and was not known to ever respond to any contacts made to it. I was surprised that such a power or force even existed throughout the galaxy, and that we could contact it. In fact, we were all surprised that it had already actually aided us that one time to find the location of the entity. Would it help us again now? Would it lend us the immense power we needed so that I could be transported to the Kin-Ty-Roo? And if it did, what was the reason for this great mystical force in helping us? If it helped thus, then what did it want? It seemed most complicated and these were only some of the thoughts that were mixing themselves in the jumble of my mind as I waited for Lord Aron and Lord Kneth to build the power of the meld to a level where they could then contact the Sacred Ku.

There was a long moment of intense silence and waiting, and then...

"Contact has been made and—accepted!" Lord Aron stated simply, but I could hear the joy in his voice. This was a major accomplishment and never an accepted thing.

From where I stood inside the mind meld ring, I could not see the vast star field I had seen before when I had been a mere spectator when Aron and his people had first been in contact with the Sacred Ku. Now all I saw from inside the ring was Lord Aron and Lord Kneth and the other elders of Kev standing around me in a circle, and then suddenly, they were gone—or more accurately—

I was gone!

I instantly found myself somewhere else.

It was hard to describe exactly where I was now. Or what it was. I found myself in a seemingly limitless dark land, flat and silent and stretching on forever and ever as far as the eye could see. There was a terrible smell of death all around me, but no bodies that I could see. In fact, there was absolutely nothing, as far as I could see, just a vast expanse of flat empty land that stretched on forever. It was incredible. I looked all around me in every direction, and in every direction it was all the same thing. I began to fear that I had been transported to the wrong place. Could that be possible? Could this be the wrong place? Did the entity snatch me, and maybe take me to another place of its own choosing? If so, then what was this place?

I was now apparently somewhere inside the Kin-Ty-Roo, deep inside the alien planet, somewhere inside the alien entity itself. Perhaps. But where? It was a puzzle wrapped within a enigma. Now all I had to do was to discover where I was and where this 'Place of Meaning' was located, and then kill a planet-size alien entity in some manner of personal combat.

I sighed deeply, this was the way it was, so there was nothing else to do but get it done. It was time to get it done!

CHAPTER 8

The Place of Meaning

Lord Aron had assured me that he and the Keven mind meld could transport me safely and directly into the area considered to be the Place of Meaning, deep within the alien entity called the Kin-Ty-Roo. That was my target destination, that strange unknown area inside the alien entity. I was supposed to be at that area now—inside the planet that made up the entity—but I could not tell what it was, or where it was—nor where *I* was.

I looked around me with concern and considerable consternation. At least there was breathable air here, but that seemed to be all there was. This did not seem right at all. The area was certainly not what I expected it to be. There was absolutely nothing at all to see anywhere around me. I could not understand that. How could that be? There was only this vast dark black expanse, an empty flat surface that went on for many miles seemingly endlessly in all directions. There were no buildings, no fortifications, nor any natural markers of any kind. There were also no living beings in sight, alien or even anything non-living. I could not discern any object that might offer the slightest meaning to any of this endless expanse of nothingness that I saw stretching out before me—because there were no objects there at all to judge any of this by. I looked around me astounded. It appeared to be there was the same nothingness here in all directions. I was surely perplexed by this—confused by what I saw here—or perhaps what I could *not* see here? I immediately grew suspicious now. What if, what I was seeing was not what was truly here? Mind masters of all types, Keven, Sindalki, and most surely this alien entity, had the power to warp and change images and perception. They could change what most of us saw to what they wanted us to see. So with that in mind, was I actually seeing what was truly here?

The suspicious thought grew in my mind. It was a dangerous notion but I could not ignore the possibility. I tried to suppress it—but could not do so. That surprised me, for I had always had complete control of my mind and my thoughts. Suddenly I realized this idea was strange to me. I wondered where this idea had come from? Then I got it. Had it come from outside my own mind, perhaps from Lord Aron, or Lord Kneth? Or perhaps it had grown from my own suspicious nature? I could not be sure and I did not overly think about it now. I had more serious matters to consider at the moment. I decided to keep one thought in mind—accept nothing here at face value.

I nodded to myself, allowing a slight grin, this surely was a fine fix to be in, for the more I thought about this possibility, the more it made sense to me. If it was true that what I was seeing was wrong, then how would I be able to see what was *truly* here? If I was able to see what was truly here, then what was it? How could I see what was hidden from my perception? I knew that Lord Aron and Lord Kneth far away back on Ares—a million or a billion miles away—could not help me now with any more overt action. I could not expect any deeper aid from them. So I was on my own. So be it! I also wondered how the heck I would get out of here and back to Ares when I was done—done with whatever I was supposed to do here. Would I ever be able to get back home? I feared not… I put that sad thought from my mind.

Lord Aron had seemed more confident about some aspects of this mission, he assured me the mind meld would be able to bring me back safely to Ares. Well, maybe. But was he right? Was that true? Would it work? However, all that was a moot point now, for I could not even test that possibility until I had completed my mission. Whatever action that mission would be, I needed to know what form my action would take if it would complete my mission. But what might that action be? It was most perplexing. I shook my head in frustrated confusion and anger. I was totally out of my depth here. I was also growing worried, time was running short, and there seemed to be nothing I could do to fight this thing. I could not even find the location of the entity. There was nothing here to fight. There seemed nowhere to go to find my enemy. There was nothing here to even examine or investigate. The area was a vast endless nothingness that seemed to go on forever. I shook my head in utter despair, this plan seemed to have been doomed to failure from the start, and I felt the sour taste of defeat in my mouth and I hated the taste. I would not accept it.

Something had to be here in this vast wasteland, some manifestation of the alien entity, something that I could find, fight and defeat. I expected that something would appear soon now that I was here. It had to.

I shook off all my negative feelings. I would not allow them to enter my mind, or interfere with my thoughts any longer. I was Jon Kirk, Earthman, Emperor of Ares, husband of the lovely Sirah. I would never go down to defeat! The hell with this all! I would find what I needed to find here! Whatever it was, it had to be here and I would find it. Something of the entity was here, I was sure of it. Something important to it. That was all I needed to know. With that in mind I withdrew my short sword and held it up in the air defiantly before me. I pointed my blade towards the sky—or that area over my head in the direction of the sky above—or whatever that area was above me.

"I am here now! Waiting! Come out and fight me!" I shouted in a defiant and furious demand. "Coward!"

Then I saw them!

They seemed to just appear instantly, suddenly.

Where they had come from I had no idea, but I certainly recognized them.

What I saw now were row after row of brave, bold, Ares warriors and fighters. They were both Greens and Blues, all armed and drawing their swords in row after row of warriors who had suddenly just appeared there in front of me—marching towards me. I was amazed at their sudden appearance. Where had they all come from? They seemed ready for battle. And there were a lot of them! Their ranks seemed to stretch on forever far away towards the horizon. They had mysteriously appeared in a sudden instant before my eyes as if out of thin air. In a heartbeat the large empty expanse before me was now full of rank upon rank of Ares fighting men, all with swords drawn and marching towards me with murder in their eyes and fighting fury in their hearts.

"What dark magic is this?" I growled tamping down my terror with the grim determination of the solid fighting man. If such was the way this fight would go, then I would make the most of it! I was ready—ready for anything!

"Come and get me!" I shouted defiantly, my sword ready for battle.

Now that action was imminent I easily shook off the fear I felt by such a terrifying vision and prepared to meet the enemy attack. I had no idea who these mysterious Greens and Blues might be, or if they were even from Ares at all. Perhaps they were just some figment of my imagination? However, that did not matter now, for I was sure that I would find out soon enough if they were real or not. I stood steady, awaiting their attack. My blade out and ready.

The warriors came at me in bunches, and soon my cold steel rang upon their own cold metal blades with resounding blaring sounds. That clanging of metal was certainly real enough, so I assumed the men must be real as well. The loud clang of clashing blades was stupendous. I admit that I was shocked by that. I had hoped these warriors would prove to be mere projections, just shadow images, probably taken from my memory—images with no substance at all. I had hoped they would disappear once I confronted them in a hard physical attack, as if they were created out of smoke or mist. Then they would melt away. That was not the case. They had actual substance, in fact, much too much substance for my taste. They were entirely real. That meant I had to do some fast thinking and some fast fighting.

The enemy warriors came at me hard and fast like true warriors of Ares and I fought them off the same way. Hard and fast. My savage blows reigned down upon them with devastating results. We were hard fought engaged now. It proved to be a furious battle. The fight was intense but I was surprised that the enemy came at me only one at a time. This I found most uncommon in battle and I could see no reason for it. Nevertheless, I fought each one of my brave enemy attackers to the death—their death! All of them that came at me soon dropped down dead from terrible wounds and savage cuts from my blade.

My sword tasted much blood that day—and my opponents went down dead—and they did bleed! I was surprised by that as well. I wondered just what I was up against here. I cut them and they bled and died, falling down to the ground into the eternal sleep of death—

even as I wondered if they had ever truly been alive in the first place? Who were they? What were they doing here? Why were they attacking me? Were they the Kin-Ty-Roo? Unfortunately, I had no time to consider these many questions now for I was lost in the fevered heat of battle.

And yet, as I fought on, my mind was spinning with curious thoughts to understand just what was going on here, though I had little time for much deep conjecture now. I was hard pressed by a constant group of opponents. I fought like a demon to stay alive and keep myself free and unharmed. So far no enemy blade had touched me. I was able to fight my attackers off so easily only because they came at me one at a time—but also because of my many years of swordsmanship and military training, added by the fact that my Earthly muscles gave me great power and stamina. I also used my Earthly speed to great advantage to run rings around my attackers, weaving a crimson path among them with my ubiquitous blade. I further used my incredible jumping ability to escape their attacks and then come in upon them from behind before they knew I was there. The results of this method of defense and attack among them proved devastating.

However the thing that seemed most strange to me was why my attackers still only seemed to come at me one at a time. That was not a natural tactic in battle. Was this some kind of ritual, or a show of respect for me? I was, after all, emperor of Ares—but this seemed too bizarre even for me to accept. I knew battle. I knew war. This was not it. It was more like some kind of game. In any true battle, I expected to be ganged upon, surrounded, then quickly put down with half a dozen blades, but that did not happen here and my attackers did not come at me that way. It was most strange. I strained my thoughts to try to figure it out.

However, I did not overly concern myself with this aspect of the fight for I was much too busy as it raged on furiously around me. My blade seemed to be everywhere, blocking each attacker and taking them down one by one. I was proud of my prowess with the blade that day. I put up a hard defense, a wall that my attackers could not breach. I kept the main group at bay, while I concentrated upon select individual attackers and quickly dispatched them. I took them down one by one. It had turned into a real bloodbath for my attackers. They were brave warriors, but senseless attackers.

The floor beneath my feet had soon grown slippery with the blood of my enemies, it shone a fine bright red now. The rest of the warriors were still held back by their vast numbers, waiting in rank upon rank, unable to get at me since their fellows were in their way blocking them. This did not last long however, for no sooner did I dispatch one warrior, than another took his place. It didn't take a genius to see the way this battle was going to end eventually, but I resolutely fought on, hard and brave, since I had no choice, but I could not fight forever. While defeat was not an opinion, victory seemed a far off thing. Nevertheless, defeat for me was never an option! So I fought on. Relentless. With every moment my mind realizing that time was running out for me—and for Ares.

I had just driven my blade deep into my latest antagonist, a big blue brute, a Vognar, who went down with a loud groan, when I suddenly heard a massive whooshing sound, as of air escaping a tightly sealed chamber.

Then instantly all the Ares warriors simply disappeared!
They were all gone!

* * * *

I looked around me in amazement. What now?

As soon as the Ares warriors disappeared the landscape suddenly transformed itself to become what appeared to be a dense tropical jungle. The heat was stifling. If I didn't know any better I would swear that I was in the back country of South Vietnam on the Earth. I looked around me in awe and confusion. This was simply impossible! And yet, it all seemed so real.

I strained my eyes to make out just what had happened but could not see more than a few dozen feet in each direction. All around me was dense jungle foliage, mighty trees, a latticework of snakelike vines, and all manner of tropical plants. Then I heard the voice and saw her!

"Jon Kirk! Help me!" she cried out in terror.

I looked behind me and saw that it was Sirah—my Sirah—dressed in traditional Ares female clothing and being dragged through a jungle pathway by four massive Blue Korta mercenary shock troop warriors.

What were *they* doing here? For a second I stood transfixed in fascination. None of this made any sense to me.

"Jon Kirk! Help me!" Sirah cried and we caught each others eyes and the connection was made. My blood surged and a violent force I had not felt in months took control over me. My beloved was in trouble—I had to save her!

I drew my sword and throwing caution to the winds ran forward to do battle to save my wife, and my empress. Two of the Kortas detached themselves from the group to meet me in combat, even as their other two comrades continued to drag Sirah away between them. I charged like a madman at these two enemy who now blocked my path, as they leveled their deadly projectile beam rifles at me. I was red hot with rage and barely thinking about any of what I was seeing transpiring here before my eyes. I knew this did not make much sense—what the hell was Sirah even doing being here? And was it really her? And why Blue Korta troops? Wasn't this the Vietnamese jungle? It did not add up. And these Blue Korta troops—weren't they now all allied with our empire—or were they?

I had no time to ponder these questions as I dodged the first couple of projectiles fired from the Korta rifles. Then I used my Earthly leg muscles to propel myself forward in a great bounding leap that instantly put me right among the two surprised troopers. My advent upon them was so sudden and unexpected they did not know how to react. I did. My sword was out and in two mad slashes I made quick work of two of my four enemies. They fell to the ground dead. I quickly whipped their blood off my sword, sheathed it, and then picked up one of the fallen Korta rifles. Then I ran towards where I saw Sirah was being dragged by the remaining two Blue Kortas. I caught them just as they were set to disappear into a wilderness of dense tropical jungle undergrowth.

"Jon Kirk! Help me!" I heard my beloved's voice cry out to me.

"I am here, Sirah!" I shouted back, and then with one great bounding leap I put myself right behind the two big Blue Kortas shock troops who were dragging my Sirah between them as they tried their best to escape my wrath.

I lifted the projectile rifle I had taken off one of the dead Kortas and fired once, then twice, and suddenly both of the enemy troopers dropped down dead. Sirah freed herself and turned back to me in an outpouring of relief and joy. I looked at her lovely face and form, full of love for me and in relief ran forward to embrace her. We hugged each other, but when I looked into her eyes she just gave me what seemed to be a most enigmatic little smile—and then she suddenly disappeared!

She was gone!

"Sirah? Sirah! Where are you? Where have you gone?" What is this?" I shouted in anger and shock at what had just happened. Where was she? What was going on? Where was Sirah?

Suddenly the area around me transformed once again, quickly morphing back to the stark flat nothingness of the Place of Meaning. The jungle—if it was even the jungle of Vietnam as it seemed it had been—and the dead Blue Kortas were all gone. Sirah was gone. The projectile rifle I still held in my hands that I had used to kill Sirah's two abductors now also disappeared from my hands. It was all gone. Everything and everyone was gone as if it had never been there at all.

"What the hell is going on here?" I spoke to myself. I had a guess as to what was going on. The alien entity was obviously taking images and memories from inside my mind, mixing them up, and placing me in these scenarios for some reason. What reason though? Was it testing me? I realized now that the Sirah I had just seen was *not* the true Sirah. For that, at least, I was grateful. My beloved must still be safe at home upon Ares. So what now? What did this all mean?

I thought on this enigma, but not for too long as barely a moment later I found the area transformed once again, with myself standing upon a long dusty plain. It was an area that appeared to be the great plain that spread out before Tarcos on Ares, and running towards me was my best friend, Sirah's brother, and the First General of my army, the noble Zaor.

"Zaor?" I stammered in shock. "Is it really you?"

"Jon Kirk! Come with me now, we must escape. They are here now! The Winged-men are coming for us!" Zaor warned me in a voice of sharp alarm.

I looked at him in astonishment. "How can this be? How can you be here?"

He ignored my words, and just pointed up above our heads to alert me to the menace that was there. I heard the loud flap of leathery wings ever before I saw the huge flying monsters. They were diving down upon us, they brandished sharp bright bladed short swords and came at us with bloody death in their beady red eyes. There were four of them. They were huge and menacing, brandishing many sharp blades.

Winged-men of Zar!

I looked at them in astonishment but stood firm. I withdrew my sword but held my ground. Waiting.

"Jon Kirk, come with me, we must escape now!" Zaor pleaded. He had his own sword drawn, standing beside me. This Zaor seemed much like the real one but I knew that he—and all this—had to be some kind of projection or illusion drawn from my mind. It could not be real—but it was reality existing upon the Physical Plane—so it probably could kill me if I was not very careful.

"No! Stop! This is all false!" I shouted grimly.

"False or not they can still kill you! You can still die, my friend," Zaor told me, pleading, trying to pull me away to safety. We were now out in the open, easy targets for the flying winged monsters to dive down at us from overhead..

"No!" I told Zaor, as I looked up defiantly into the sky—and saw the red sunned sky of Ares and her twin moons. I ignored the Winged-men attackers. No! I am not playing this game any longer. Alien entity—come out and show yourself! Your true self! I dare you!"

There was no reply to my plea by the alien entity.

Then the four Winged-men monsters were upon us diving down at us swinging vicious sharp blades that could cut our heads off in a single furious slash. I ducked down, then struck back, my blade clanging against their own. Zaor fought back too, his sword cutting a swath through the flying fiends and knocking their swords away from us. The enemy moved off, regrouped and then came in closer. Zaor and I, now standing back to back, fought off the winged beasts as best we could, as they continued to come at us from above. It was a good strategy, however we were too open to their attack to defeat them all, but I refused to run or hide from them.

Zaor and I fought on. I knocked the sword away from one attacker, and in that moment I was able to slip my blade under the guard of a second adversary and stab him in the chest. My sword went in deep into the winged monster and suddenly he flapped wildly, uncontrollably, and then fell out of the sky to hit the ground and die at my feet. That meant we had only three enemies left.

I had a moment now to quickly think this through. I had to make some sense out of all that was happening. What was Zaor doing here? Was he not just another fake image, as Sirah had been? I was sure he was. He could not be real.

"Who are you?" I demanded of Zaor now.

"You know who I am, Jon Kirk. I am Zoar," he replied simply, as we continued to furiously fight our enemies who had attacked us once more.

"No you are not! You are a projection, or some image taken from my mind. You are not the true Zaor. Zaor could not be here. Who are you?" I demanded in a loud growl, almost ready to turn my blade upon him.

"Fight, Jon Kirk, we need to defeat these winged monsters," the man who was Zaor, but was *not* Zaor, said to me.

I turned to look again at him during a break in the attack. It was when the three remaining enemy had flown high above us to begin another crash dive upon us to cut us down. I looked into Zaor's eyes and demanded once more, "Who are you?"

"I am Zaor, your best friend," he replied simply.

"No, you are not," I replied, then I added, "Are you the entity? Are you this Kin-Ty-Roo, or some manifestation of it?"

Zaor gave me the same enigmatic smile I had recently seen upon Sirah's face, then suddenly he and the Winged-men just disappeared. Even the body of the dead Winged-man who lay motionless at my feet just disappeared. Zaor was gone. The locale of the plains of Tarcos on Ares was gone now as well.

It was all gone!

* * * *

I found myself back in the vast nothingness of the Place of Meaning. The Place of Meaning, indeed. I wondered just what it all really did mean. All these games. Was the alien entity testing me? If so, why? What was this all about? I could not figure it out, but someone or something was certainly creating and controlling these events for some definite reason. I just wished I could figure it out. I also wished that I would be able to find my way back home to Ares, but I felt that there was something more that I needed yet to do here. I wondered what that could be?

I looked around me astonished by this sudden turn of events, but very thankful that I had evidently survived them. I wondered what had precipitated all these images and scenarios, but figured that whoever—or whatever—was controlling events here had decided upon a different plan for me, or some other mode of attack. I wondered what was coming next. I was astonished but thankful by what had transpired and that for now, my enemies were gone. And I knew now that even the Sirah and Zaor I had met here had not been real. They were all some form of the enemy, and all had disappeared as mysteriously as they had appeared. It was uncanny, yet I remained sharp and alert, my sword out and ready for whatever would come next.

What really was going on here? What was the purpose of all this? Was this some kind of test? Or was I being set up in some manner of battle for the entity to observe me, or to see what I was made of in an effort to better defeat me? It seemed incomprehensible—but quite often the ways of aliens could be most incomprehensible. I looked around and wondered what was to come? The emptiness around me was stark, limitless and unfathomable.

"Talk to me! Make yourself known!" I loudly demanded in anger, but there was no reply.

I knew there would be no reply.

I could not understand this strange activity. The warriors could have easily had me dead to rights—eventually. I knew in our battle it was but a matter of time before they would prevail against me if this were real life. If they had been serious to defeat me in battle. They certainly had the numbers. But then again, perhaps they could not defeat me—for it seemed to me that they did not press their attack to actually win! It was as if they did not want to win. I wondered about that and what it might mean. And what of Sirah and Zaor? What was their purpose in being here? Obviously to motivate me in some way, but how and why? It seemed that I was being tested or investigated. But again, why? I knew the alien entity was observing all of this. I thought it through as I continued to scan the area around me intently looking for any sign of—anything.

The area had gone back to the large empty flat expanse that it had appeared as when I had first arrived in this strangest of places. The dead bodies of all the warriors I had killed in battle were gone. So was even any evidence of their blood, which I had shed in such large abundance. Where had they gone? Where had Sirah and Zaor gone? Where was all the blood that had been shed and that had pooled so widely upon the floor? Something mysterious was up in this most mysterious of places.

Nonetheless, I did not allow anything to deter me. These actions only made my resolve to figure out this puzzle more determined. I sheathed my sword. My mind did not accept all of what I had seen here any longer. I did not accept what I was seeing with my eyes. I would not accept any of it!

"This is a sham! *You* are a sham!" I shouted defiantly. "Kin-Ty-Roo!"

I walked on.

I looked around me furious in anger now. I knew I was being played with and I did not like it.

"Show yourself you coward!" I barked in anger. "Enough of your useless stupid games!"

There was no answer as I expected, but I did not let that deter me either. The Kin-Ty-roo was not some sinister master villain like Lord Doom had been, it was a seemingly all-powerful alien entity of vast power and incomprehensible intentions. It was even said to be some kind of a god. If that was true that could really complicate things. I wondered just what it was up to. I wondered just where this so-called Place of Meaning might be located. Was this it? It seemed unlikely—a vast nothingness—there seemed no logical reason for it—and yet…?

Then I laughed at the irony, realizing that while I was looking for something that was hidden here—this must indeed be my intended target, the Place of Meaning, and that perhaps it appeared exactly as I was seeing it. Now that made a difference. It was all just nothingness. That got me thinking. So perhaps it was no illusion—it was all real, and it was just as it appeared to be? It had to be. It was most strange, but one thing I have learned in my life upon Ares and the worlds out here in the vastness of outer space, is that alien ways are often *very* alien. Even incompressible. The so-called Place of Meaning was this entire area and in reality it was as I plainly saw it. It appeared to be nothing and nothingness— and that is just what it was—perhaps much like the entity itself? And yet, it seemed it could be transformed into anything by the powers of the entity, if it so desired. That was quite interesting to me.

Lord Aron and Lord Kneth had been correct, they had sent me to the proper location. I trusted them. I had been looking for a more substantial place, a special place within this area based upon my own assumptions of what such a control center might look like—but they had been human assumptions. Instead, the truth was that the entire area was the Place of Meaning. Or so I surmised and believed it to be now. If that was true, then just what did it mean? I feared I would go crazy trying to figure it out—but figure it out I would!

I took a deep breath and thought about all I had encountered and seen since I had first appeared here. I reconsidered everything I had seen and done here more carefully. If what I surmised was really true, then what did it actually mean? I thought it through. I walked onward, looking down at my feet, as I took step after step, noticing my boots and my feet as I walked upon the black shiny floor, and I wondered about it. That floor. I looked at it more closely and began to wonder about it even more. I realized that it seemed quite strange. It was not made of ground or dirt, nor grass or sward. It was not created out of cement or steel, nor metal of any kind. It was a floor certainly, but that was only the way I thought of it. Perhaps it was something else? Something more? Or something different? That meant I might have to look at it in a different way. I did. I examined it closely and I noticed that it appeared to be made of some kind of firm flesh or tissue, and that got me to really wondering. I looked at the floor most carefully now and slowly nodded my head. Here was something to look into more seriously.

I quickly withdrew my sword. The Place of Meaning? We would surely see about that. I deftly plunged the point of my blade deeply into the floor and it gave way as my blade sunk downward into it. I plunged my blade in deeper, as far as it would go. When I pulled out my blade I noticed a dark viscous fluid run out from the opening made by my blade. It looked terrible. It smelled bad. I looked at it closely and a grim smile came to my face.

"You bleed! Though not the true red blood as true life does, you do bleed! And if you bleed, I can make you bleed a river!" I cried in rage and then I set to work.

I quickly struck the area again and opened up three more large wounds, plunging my blade point deep into the openings and causing massive streams of what I could only think of as the blood of this alien thing to flow outward. It was like black sludge. It poured out in a stream.

It was bleeding!

I was hurting it!

That seemed a good thing.

I took my sword and continued to cut with frantic haste deep into the substance that made up the floor below my feet and then slashed across it to rend a large two foot long gash that opened up the area quite nicely. The result of these sword cuts was extraordinary. The amount of dark viscous fluid that now poured out of the ground, actually squirting out like a small oil geyser now began to cover the area in a large dark slick. It bubbled out like sludge. The odor was terrible. The appearance was ghastly. I only nodded grimly, this was certainly working and inflicting damage upon the enemy entity so I continued my cutting work with renewed relish.

I attacked the thing hard, slashing and cutting into the floor or wall or whatever it was, my sword inflicting terrible damage upon the entity—or at least I hoped that I was. I truly had no way to know how my actions were affecting the entity, but I went with my intuition and with what my heart was telling me. What I was doing could not be a good thing for any enemy. So I fought against the thing relentlessly. I continued my cutting, tearing and rending. Deep sword strokes. The area was now a thick fluid mess that stank terrible, but I continued cutting it to ribbons as long as I could do so. The more damage I did to the entity—or to this part of the entity—the more I knew I must be causing it severe distress. Or so I hoped.

It was not soon after that when I felt a sudden massive shock.

It was like a mini earthquake, a heavy shuddering jolt that threw me backwards and seemed like it was spreading throughout the entire area of this so-called Place of Meaning. Perhaps through the entire planet itself?

I stood up and continued my work and as a result the shuddering grew more serious and violent. I knew I was getting somewhere now. Something was certainly happening. It was difficult for me to keep my balance, hard to stand on my feet, but I did so, and I continued using my sword to cut and hurt the beast, plunging it down deeply into the area beneath my feet. Was this the very heart of the entity? I had no way of knowing, but I knew this, my actions were hurting it. I was causing it pain and I was doing it damage. That was good and so I continued.

I shouted in rage as I worked, knowing now that this was what I had been sent here to do—to put pain to the Kin-Ty-Roo and hopefully damage it. I made another deep incision when I instantly felt myself pulled in a wild whirling upward motion. Some force had taken control of me and was pulling me upwards—to where I did not know. Why this was happening I did not know. Had the entity taken control of me somehow? Was it now going to take its revenge on me for the pain I had inflicted upon it?

So be it!

I steeled my nerves and waited as I was pulled up higher in a whirlwind of utter chaos—my hand holding on for dear life tightly to the pommel of my sword—for if this was the end, I was determined to sell my life dearly.

In the blink of an eye everything changed!

* * * *

I now found myself standing in the center of the mind meld circle back on Ares.

I looked around me and saw the faces of Lord Aron, Lord Kneth, and all the other Keven mind masters, each one of the venerable sages standing around me in curious attention.

I had returned to Ares!

"Jon Kirk, it is good to have you back among us," Lord Aron said to me, allowing a slight smile that I returned with a deep breath of sheer utter relief. I was back! Back on Ares! Somehow, Lord Aron and his team had been able to transport me back to Ares! They had kept their word. I wondered how they had been able to do it.

"It is good to be back, Aron, but what happened?" I asked astounded, as Sirah, Zaor and the others who were there rushed over to welcome me.

"It appears you did something—whatever needed to be done—to confound the entity. Whatever it was that needed to be done, you did it," Lord Kneth told me in a serious but curious tone.

I simply shook my head, not at all sure of what the meaning of what I had done, actually was. I shrugged and told them so, "I appeared there, just as you sent me, and there was a vast nothingness. Then some Ares warriors appeared and I fought them off. The area is a endless flat land that seemed to go on forever. That did not seem to make much difference to anything that happened there. After the warriors disappeared I fought some others, Blue Kortas and even Winged-men, I even saw images of Sirah, and you, Zaor, and then I tried something else. It was mostly out of sheer frustration and anger. All I did was plunge my sword blade deeply into the floor—and I continued to do so in anger and frustration. It was only then that I noticed a dark fluid bleeding out of the great gashes I had made— wounds into the entity, I guess—so I just continued to do this again and again. I kept at it. It seemed to cause a violent reaction from the entity. I believe that I was causing it some pain."

"Great pain, I would say. That area was not the floor," Lord Kneth told me explaining what I had seen and where I had been within the entity. "It is a special part of the entity, an intimate area that you entered unexpectedly and caused great damage. That damage you did to it ended up helping us very much, for you weakened the powers of the creature."

"Jon Kirk, your actions obviously were unexpected and weakened the entity, or caused it severe distress. The alien entity known as the Kin-Ty-Roo—the entire planet—was placed in some form of convulsive chaos through your actions. It was only then that we could act," Aron The Eldest added. "And we did!"

I looked at the Keven mind master and the Sindalki lord shaking my head in abject wonder and surprise, "All I did was use my sword to stab the floor, or wall, or whatever it was, in the huge room I was trapped in. It was more out of rage and frustration than any actual plan that I had in mind—for in fact I had no plan at that point."

"Perhaps not, but you acted on instinct and your instinct was correct," Lord Aron told me.

I nodded thoughtfully, "Yes, I imagine so. That area seemed the only place where I could plunge my weapon into the thing. So I did! And I did get a reaction. So I continued to do it! Once I saw that my actions caused the entity to leak that oily dark vile smelling fluid—I knew I had hit something that was important—so I kept at it!"

"Yes, dark vile fluid like that seems appropriate coming from such an evil thing. Your actions caused it to weaken, and that allowed us to place the entity through our mind meld—with the help of the Sacred Ku—into a compound stasis," Lord Aron told me now with pride.

"In stasis? An entire planet? Or an entire planet-sized entity?" I asked incredulous. Was it possible? This kind of super science and mind master power was far above the head of a simple fighting man such as myself. However, I still appreciated it.

"It is not a planet, though it is the size of one, it is just an extremely large alien entity. However, with the help of the Sacred Ku, and using our mind powers, combined with Ras-noor's marvelous machines, we were able to temporarily overcome the power of the entity and place it in a controlled compound stasis. It now seems to be moribund. Perhaps sleeping? Or in some similar reduced energy state? In any case it is silent. Or so we think. Or so we hope. It is surrounded by a force field that is powered by Ras-noor's magnificent machines and augmented by the controlling force of the Sacred Ku. The force of the Sacred Ku has set forth its force to collaborate with our own powers now and that has caused a stalemate for the entity. Or so we believe. We can not be certain on any of this, of course. We know now that it has stopped its voracious appetite. It is no longer feeding, it has stopped absorbing worlds and planets, or any form of matter or energy that comes anywhere near it. It has stopped its feeding. For now," Lord Kneth told me, hopeful victory with dire suspicion showing mixed in his features.

I nodded, taking in all I had just heard with amazing awe, added to by my own deep suspicion about all this. I looked around me at all present there in that room and they each seemed to be happy with what I had accomplished. I was not even sure I had accomplished anything of merit, but they seemed to think so, and if what I had done hurt the creature, or if I had weakened it enough to enable it to be held in stasis, then I was happy. I was all for it. So far so good, I thought. What next now?

"Now is the time to strike, Jon Kirk!" I heard a voice speak up from the fringes of the crowd and I saw that it was Crooch. He walked forward and told me in a firm voice, "Kill it now! Send in the Grand Fleet! Destroy it, explode it!"

I looked back at Crooch and then looked over towards Zaor, who nodded his head in agreement. As did Sahn-jor.

Crooch's advice seemed to be quite popular among my closest advisors and I could not deny it made sense. Especially now. I even agreed with him. Right now seemed to offer the opportunity we had hoped for. Hit the entity right away—hard—while it was weak and helpless! If it was truly weak and helpless? I had my doubts about that however—for this was an entity the size of an entire planet—and it was an alien thing that many said was as mighty as a god. Or perhaps it might even be some kind of god! We had no idea what we were dealing with here. Since I was the only one who had been within the entity, I had many doubts and questions about it. These all gave me great cause for concern.

I shook my head, trying to clear my thoughts on the matter, and as ever looked to my beloved wife, Sirah, for her wise advice. "What do you say, my love?"

She looked deeply into my eyes, smiled, overjoyed that I had returned to her, and little Alun. "Do what you think best, my love. You do have options."

I looked at her carefully and thought over her words. My wife was a smart woman and I always listened to her wise counsel. However, I could not see exactly what she meant, so I asked her, "What… options?"

"Well, I—I think Ras-noor and the others should tell you about them. We discussed them while you were gone—inside that thing— in anticipation of your return."

"In anticipation of my return?" I asked with a wide grin. "My return was not a sure thing at all. In fact, I thought my mission was going to end in failure and death."

Sirah just gave me a wide grin followed by a deep kiss. Then she said, "Jon Kirk, you give yourself so little credit. I knew it was a sure thing you would come back to us, so I had your ministers and advisors discuss options for you to consider upon your return."

"Hah!" I rang out with a lusty laugh, taking her in my arms holding her to me tightly, as I smothered her lips with hot kisses. "You are too much!"

"But not too much for you, my love!" she whispered softly in my ear.

I had to agree with that as I kissed her again.

CHAPTER 9

Options

I never considered that there could be options in dealing with an entity such as the Kin-Ty-Roo. How could such a thing even be possible? I figured that it was either kill it—or be killed by it! It was that simple. I was lucky and thankful that somehow Lord Aron and Lord Kneth had been able to place the alien entity in some kind of contained stasis prison—though how they achieved it—even after they and Ras-noor explained the process to me—I did not completely understand. It was all super scientific Ancient Ares advancements and mental mind master gymnastics to me. And as for the Sacred Ku—that was an even more mysterious elemental force which I had no idea what to make of. I assume it was some sort of Universal Mind, or some form of intergalactic cosmic consciousness—all way too complicated for me to understand. These complex mystical and spiritual powers were far over my head, for I was just a simple fighting man. And proud of it! I was certainly no scientist nor mind master, though my Earthly origin did allow me certain powers here on Ares that the natives did not possess. My Earthly powers of being an outworlder even made me immune to some mind master manipulations. I was nevertheless thankful that I had such talented people around me to count on for their help in this war, and the weapons we had of use to us now from what the Sindalki called the Three Forms of Power.

"So now, my friends," I asked everyone once we were all seated in our war council around a large table in the Great Hall in the imperial palace in Tarcos. "we seem to have options to deal with this entity—or so I have been informed. That is good. What might they be?"

Ras-noor looked at Aron The Eldest, who drew our gaze to Lord Kneth. The Sindalki sage nodded, then stood up to address the members of the council.

"It is an interesting conundrum that has been placed before us, My Emperor," Lord Kneth began in a calm deliberative tone. "A deadly and seemingly all-powerful alien entity—perhaps in some ways even as powerful as a god. Now we have to deal with it before it destroys us all. At present we have but temporarily dealt with it, placing it in compound stasis, but how long that can hold it under control is anyone's guess. I do not agree with some here that its imprisonment can last very long. The creature is far too powerful and may be able to eventually resist anything we can do to stop it."

It was grim news and got me thinking. I looked at the Sindalki and said, "I agree, but what can we do about it?"

Aron the Eldest stood up then, looked at the faces of all the leaders of the empire seated around that huge table, "We have some alternatives. We can keep it held in stasis for as long as we are able to do so. I believe this is our weakest option, as I agree with Lord Kneth, the entity is much too powerful to be detained this way for any long period of time."

"Well how long do we have then? How much time?" I asked the key question that all there wanted to know.

The venerable Keven leader merely shrugged, "Who can say for certain. I believe that at any moment the entity could breach the stasis field and set itself free. Or perhaps, it may be held there helpless for a manner of years? Who can truly know."

I nodded gravely, it was certainly deep food for though and I hated the ambiguity of it all. Trouble seemed to be on the way once again. "All right, then give me the other options."

Zaor stood up now, the First General and leader of the empire's military. He looked at me firmly, "Jon Kirk, I say we take the fleet, surround this planet—this Kin-Ty-Roo thing—or whatever it is—and blast it into oblivion. Our death ray weapons and projectile beams from half a hundred warships will make a quick end to it. That is the only way to ensure we kill it completely. We use every weapon we have to utterly vaporize it. We need to leave no doubt that this thing is destroyed completely."

I nodded at Zaor, his counsel seemed to be correct. Thoughtful. It made sense. It was certainly a warrior's solution to such a problem. There did not seem to be any other way to deal with the menace, and that troubled me for some reason I could not explain. And the fact that I could not explain it, even troubled me more. Something was up and I did not like it. But what? What was it that bothered me about the prospect of destroying this entity?

"Ah, hum!" Ras-noor cleared his throat to get my attention, then he stood and faced me directly.

"Yes, my friend?"

"There is a third alternative. Well actually, there are a total of four or five of them—but I will only now speak of a possible third option."

"Go on," I urged curious. Everyone looked at the old scientist now.

"I propose we do to the entity, what we did with you weeks ago to save the planet Earth. We send it on a trip back in time. We have solved the problem of time travel and used it effectively in that one instance. Now we have augmented our power since your visit to the past to confront Lord Doom and save the Earth from destruction. Now I propose we send the entity backwards in time—*very far* back in time—to the very beginning of the universe. Far away from here and now. We have that knowledge —we have that ability now—let us use it!"

I looked closely at wily old Ras-noor, "Is such a thing possible? I mean, on that kind of massive scale? I was just one man that you sent back in time—and it was a tricky thing to do even then. That thing is as big as a planet."

"Yes, I believe it is possible, Jon Kirk."

I thought seriously upon the matter. It would get rid of the entity for good. Or so I was told. It seemed an idea with much merit to it and I could see that it had some real benefit to solving our problem, but I had my doubts as well.

Aron The Eldest quickly interjected, "My Emperor, Ras-noor is an esteemed scientist whose knowledge of the Ancients of Ares, and *The Book of Kor*, is well known by all here. He has unlocked the secret of time travel with Lord Kneth, and through his work we may be able to perform such a mission even to transporting the entity. However, this entity is seemingly all-powerful, it may be only temporarily immobile. In fact, it may have its own way of traveling the pathways of time. We are not sure. But if that is the case…"

Lord Aron left the implication unsaid but I knew that his concerns were valid and perhaps crucial.

"So in other words this entity might be able to thwart our attempt to transport it into the past?" I asked seeking input from my nobles and lords.

"Perhaps. Or worse, it may be able to come back from the past and reappear in our own time, and if so, who knows what additional knowledge and power it will have gained through its travels. The damage it could inflict in our present time and among our allied worlds would be incalculable."

I looked at the Keven mind master and grimaced. It certainly seemed to place us in a difficult position. I knew all there were looking for me to make a decision, quick and heavy action would certainly do the trick now, but I held off for some reason I could not quite explain.

Lord Aron suddenly added most carefully, showing a dark grim look to his face that I did not like. "In my opinion, the entity is too much of a mystery for us to use this option to deal with it. Suppose, let us say, that it does not presently have the knowledge of time travel. I believe this to be the case because we have seen no evidence of any use by it yet—but perhaps through our own use of time travel against it, the entity could gain that knowledge? That would be disastrous. Then we would be in deeper trouble than before, and it might be able to travel the timelines at will. The damage it could do to us would be unimaginable."

There was loud and confusing turmoil throughout the chamber. Fear on the faces of many there and deep concern on even the most sensible and grounded of my advisors and ministers. Many hoped for a quick solution to the problem of the entity and this idea seemed to be it. I could not blame them but I called for calm and silence.

Lord Aron's words posed a most terrifying thought to me. I did not overly like this option, but I decided to keep it on the back burner for now—who knew what the future would hold. Events were so fluid and surprising that it was difficult to know how best to deal with this monster at any given moment.

"Well, then, setting that aside for now, are there any more options on how we can handle this entity?" I asked my ministers and advisors, my generals, officers, and the other leaders of the empire I now ruled. All of my inner circle.

There was silence around the large table and throughout the huge hall that was deafening in its implications. It did not bode well.

I looked around me at the faces of all who were there but there was not much in the way of anything new in our attempt to deal with the entity, other than Zaor's suggestion of sending the fleet to bomb it into oblivion. I was all for this—but I felt that caution was needed here more than ever, before we acted. I had an inkling that not all was as it seemed. So I waited. I hoped we had enough time to make some sense of all this and perhaps obtain more facts and information.

Ras-noor finally stood up, "There are fourth and fifth options that may be of some value. At least I believe they should be mentioned here."

"That is fine, what are they, Ras-noor?"

The wily old scientist looked around the room, "Well, we may be able to send a group of warriors into this Place of Meaning within the entity to do much more extensive damage to it than you did before."

I nodded slowly, "Possible, I imagine, but not very practical. The thing will surely have counter measures prepared now. I believe the only reason I was able to be successful in my recent mission there was because my appearance inside the being, and my damage to it, had been so unexpected. The entity was not prepared for such an attack in that most sensitive location. Certainly not there. At least that is what common sense dictates. It will not be unprepared again. It was weakened as a result of my attack, and its weakness enabled the stasis field to take hold. I do not believe we will have that opportunity again."

"Lord Aron and I are in agreement in that theory, Jon Kirk," Lord Kneth spoke up in a firm voice. Then he added in a careful, measured tone, "However, you sell yourself short. This entity is a monster of incalculable power, I believe it was something special about you—and *you* alone—that allowed you to harm it. No one else could succeed in such a mission. The very tests you were given show us this plainly."

Ras-noor nodded, "I agree, a most plausible possibility, but I felt I should put it forward nevertheless. I also do not feel it will be successful for us to send any other warriors within it to fight it."

"Of course," I replied accepting their advice, seeming to know in my heart that they were correct, "and now, your fifth option?"

Ras-noor shook his head and shrugged, "Some form of communication with the entity, perhaps?"

"To what end?"

"Well, perhaps to see if there is a possibility that we can co-exist peacefully. I admit it is a far off hope, perhaps even a forlorn hope, but I believe in putting forward to you all options available, no matter how slim may be their success." Ras-noor stated.

I looked at my friend most dubiously. This would not do.

"That option will never work with such a thing!" Sahn-jor spoke up firmly before I could reply, and the tone of his opposition to this plan surprised me, for he was the most peaceful and peace-seeking member of all the leaders of the empire.

"I thank you both. Lord Aron, what do you say to this last option?"

"Impossible, Jon Kirk. The entity exists entirely to feed. It is as simple as that," he said shaking his head meaningfully. "There can be no negotiation with it."

"And yet it has stopped feeding." I stated carefully, for this latest important news had just come to us.

"Yes, it has stopped feeding, at least temporarily."

"So Lord Aron, what do you see as the reason for that?"

The Keven mind master only nodded thoughtfully, he was as perplexed by this turn of events as was I, "Unknown. Perhaps the stasis field is interfering with its ability to absorb matter? I do not know. Perhaps it is satiated and does not need to feed any longer?"

I looked at Lord Aron sharply, wondering what that might mean, seeking further explanation.

The Keven shook his head helplessly, "I have no information to give you on that, Jon Kirk. Vision is closed to us in that area. I am sorry."

I nodded deeply, it seemed par for the course when dealing with the entity. I looked at Lord Aron closely, "Yes, I have heard it has stopped its feeding, but can anyone here tell me why it feeds? If in fact, it exists to feed, why does it exist to feed? What is behind its actions, or what is its goal, if any?"

No one spoke a word, for no one there knew the answer. Only Crooch spoke up once again, intense and firm, "Jon Kirk, I beg of you once more, destroy it immediately before it destroys us all!"

There was quite a lot of agreement from many around that table for Crooch's course of action. I could not deny the reality of his words, but I still felt I needed to make sure I made the right decision here, and that a right decision, might not be what seemed to be right as far as the facts as we knew them. There was something that seemed wrong to me here, something hidden. I was very suspicious of everything I was hearing, and always the question nagged at me, what could be the goal of such an all-powerful entity?

CHAPTER 10

The Dark Tide

Of the five options presented to me for dealing with the alien entity, I rejected two immediately out of hand. Another attack in the Place of Meaning within the entity would not work and I would only be dealing the fighting men I sent there a terrible death sentence.

As for the fifth option? I knew there could be no negotiation with such a monster.

That left us with three highly unlikely and most probably unsuccessful modes of operation. Keeping the thing in stasis for as long as possible seemed only a stop-gap measure useful only until it escaped. And at some point, at some time, it would surely escape. At least I believed that to be the case. It had to be. Then we would have to deal with it at that time, which was hardly a viable option. This plan was not proactive enough for me and not really acceptable. However, who knew how long the thing might remain helpless and held in stasis? Would it be for a thousand more *seconds*—or a thousand more *years*? We had no way of knowing, and that was not acceptable to me either.

Destroying the entity outright with our fleet—if such an action was even possible— and I was not entirely certain that we had the power to do that, even though it seemed to be the wisest course— might not work either. Who knew for sure? Nothing was a certainty. It was a devilish Hobson's choice if ever there was one. Perhaps it would work? I was not so sure.

However, there was also the option of sending the entity back in time. If that was, in fact, actually possible. This plan seemed too tricky and fraught with what could be some dangerous unintended complications. I did not like this idea very much and was most leery of attempting it.

"It is certainly a trio of dark choices, My Emperor. We are set adrift upon a dark tide with no markers or maps to guide us in what we must do," Aron the Eldest told me later.

I nodded with dark resignation, it certainly seemed that way.

"What shall we do?" Lord Aron asked me.

"Zaor, what of the rest of the Enemy Empire fleet? This Kin-Ty-roo controls a massive fleet of warships —a much larger fleet with many more ships than were ever controlled by Lord Doom. Doom's ships are ours now after his defeat, their crews ours now as well. They have all come over to our side and sworn allegiance. However, there is a much more serious problem. The remainder of the alien entity fleet with least one thousand warships remaining and unaccounted for. What has happened to them?"

Lord Aron was silent, as he and I were thinking it through. We knew this to be a serious problem that we had to somehow deal with soon.

Zaor was quiet. I could tell he did not like this situation.

I shook my head, then added, "There are also many planets, alien races, conquered worlds still loyal to the entity. Their inhabitants are terrified of it and hence unwilling to aid us. Their fear is a physical thing with them. So why are they not engaged in battle against us now? It is almost as if they are being held back, or have been ordered off. I can not understand this. I would think the enemy would send in all their warships to immediately destroy Ares, much as Lord Doom tried to do—they still have a massive and deadly fleet. We may not even be able to stand up against them. If they do attack Ares we are in trouble. And here is something else. Why would they not use that massive fleet to set free their entity master from the stasis field. They apparently have done neither of these actions. Why?"

"Inaction by the enemy causes me concern," Zaor said briskly. He nodded, looked around the room at all the faces of the members of the empire—various beings of all races and aliens of every type. Each being there representing their home world and their 'people'— and I use the word advisedly for while mostly humanoid beings, many were certainly not 'people' in any way that I thought of people from Earth. However, all were members of the empire I served, and all were equal and valued members of that empire and would have our respect and protection.

I looked once more at Zaor, as First General of the Army of the empire he was the man I turned to when I needed advice on military and war matters.

"My Emperor, Jon Kirk, the Enemy Empire fleet has seemingly disappeared. It is a grouping of more than one thousand warships, but it seems to have gone away. It has simply vanished from the our region of the Known Universe. It is not anywhere in the vicinity of the entity, and it is not in the vicinity of any of the worlds of our empire, including Ares —nor anywhere in known space, including The Empty Quarter. This vast Enemy Empire fleet of the Kin-Ty-Roo has simply disappeared and we do not know where it is."

I looked at Zaor and could not hide my incredulousness at this latest mystery. I looked at everyone else around the table, seeking answers. I demanded, "Where did the Enemy Empire fleet go? Where are those damn warships!"

There was stunned silence for a long moment.

Ras-noor finally looked up at me, shook his head, "This entity is from another galaxy certainly—or perhaps even a different universe or perhaps some other dimension of time or space altogether. It is difficult to tell which it may be. Perhaps it has sent the fleet back where it has come from for some reason?"

"For what reason?" I asked, short-tempered now.

Ras-noor only shrugged and no one else answered my question, which I found most vexing.

"It has that kind of power?" I asked in a low tone tinged with awe. I would not allow fear to creep into my voice, nor my thoughts, but this was a mystery that must be cleared up and dealt with immediately.

"Yes, perhaps," Ras-noor replied softly. However, he did not seem to be so sure about what he said at all. How could he be?

"Perhaps the entity has simply absorbed the ships of its own fleet?" Zaor put forth hopefully. "Devoured them all, much as it has done to the many suns and planets it has encountered in The Empty Quarter?"

"That could be," Gorm growled, also allowing for some hope to enter his words.

I shook my head firmly negative at this idea, "No, that can not be it. I can not believe that possibility. Such an entity would never do such a thing. It does not make sense."

"Then where are the enemy warships?" Zaor asked the question uppermost in all our minds.

I could not answer that question and it irked me greatly. They were surely somewhere. Had they gone back home? If so, where was home? Were they in hiding, bidding their time even now, before they struck us? Or had the entity truly devoured them? That possibility seemed impossible to me, but the one thing I had learned since coming to Ares is that the impossible is always possible given the right circumstances.

Lord Aron then spoke up voicing a dire prediction, "We must remember that in its own sphere of reality, Jon Kirk, this entity—this Kin-Ty-Roo—may be looked upon as some kind of a god. If that is true then that possibility changes everything."

I darted a look at the Keven mind master, "You're not telling me that this thing is—God!"

"No! Certainly not!" Lord Aron replied aghast at my question, and I could see that he was even insulted that I would intimate he had suggested such a thing. Then he relaxed and allowed a slim smile, "Jon Kirk, there is only one creator of everything. One God! I am merely trying to explain some things that I saw in Crooch's mind that I have recently thought long upon. I believe that the entity, in its own universe may be thought to be a god, and it may, in fact, believe itself to be a god. It certainly has great—one might almost say even—god-like powers."

"All right, so now what?" I asked with care, for it appeared things seemed to be getting worse by the minute. Were we truly in a battle with some kind of a god? I asked Lord Aron, "What does this mean exactly?

Lord Aron shook his head in thoughtful concern.

Lord Kneth, the last of the Sindalki spoke up then, "I have lately studied the old texts. If this being is one of the lesser gods, or believes itself to be some type of a god, then we must deal with it accordingly, at least as far as Sindalki custom and history tells us. Our ancient laws are clear on this matter and may be able to assist us here."

"All right," I prompted the proud Sindalki, "and what exactly does that mean, Lord Kneth?"

"Jon Kirk, it is actually quite simple, according to the ancient Sindalki laws and texts—laws old before my people ever were contacted by the Ancients of Ares, texts written before even the Ancients of Ares were born—there is one way to deal with such a force. The long ago words are clear to us—even today—a god can only be killed—by another god."

I shook my head in despair and frustration at this confusing and esoteric information. What did it mean? It all seemed to be some form of mystical gobbledygook to me. What was he telling me? Could it be true? I had to admit that I was skeptical, but I was an Earthman, an outworlder, and I had seen many strange and remarkable things since I had first come to Ares. In truth, I knew now, that almost anything was possible. And even the impossible could be plausible given the right conditions. The implications were giving me a headache.

I sighed and slowly spoke up, "Well, that does not do us any good. We do not seem to have any other god here that we can use to fight the entity— nor any god that is available and is on our side to do the deed."

I though briefly of the Sacred Ku, but that was not a being, not any type of god at all, just some primal cosmic force. Uncontrollable and enigmatic. It would not do.

I was shocked when I noticed that many of the faces in that chamber were now turned towards me. They had a look on their faces that showed desperate hope. I heard some of them mutter my name in a low, but growing whisper. I looked back at them in shock, shaking my head in obvious annoyance at what was happening. Now what were they thinking? What were they up to?

Gorm of Gorm pointed towards me with a big wide grin, loudly chanting, "Jon Kirk! Jon Kirk! Jon Kirk!"

I looked at the huge alien warrior in utter surprise, and even disdain, but others there also looked at me as they took up his chant and I saw a sudden glow come in their eyes. I shook my head, this seemed to be getting out of hand, and I knew I had to put a stop to it before it got way out of the realm of all reason.

"No! No! No! Do not even think it!" I stated with some anger and force now. I was angry by the very thought of what they seemed to be thinking, for if I read their thoughts correctly... This was so wrong, it was sheer blasphemy. It was…

"Jon Kirk…" Lord Aron asked softly.

"I am sorry, I can not accept this! I will not accept this!"

"No, Jon Kirk, you mistake the meaning of the people here and their loyalty to you. You also mistake Lord Kneth's words in what he tells us the old texts say," Lord Aron advised me quietly, calmly. He gave me a warm reassuring smile that made me feel somewhat better about what he was saying. "Look at it this way, My Emperor. This entity *believes* itself to be a god. That is just the reality of the situation from *its* viewpoint. Of course we do not believe it—but *it* does! So let us use that knowledge against it. So we believe that it somehow—and I am now quite sure of this though I can not imagine why—it *believes* that *you* are also some type of a god."

I just laughed out loud at the ridiculousness of that utter bit of malarkey, "Well, it is just silly and certainly not true! That is just a bunch of bunk! If the entity believes such utter nonsense it is much confused and it has another thing coming, let me tell you!"

"But Jon Kirk…?" Lord Aron prompted.

"No! Absolutely not!" I barked in annoyance now, which I was not ashamed to show before all the leaders of the empire in that room. "We all know that this god theory is untrue and more so, it is blasphemous, and I will have none of it!"

"Most laudatory, My Emperor," Lord Kneth said simply with an ironic gleam in his coal black eyes. I could not tell if he was being honest or cynical. He could be a most cynical fellow at times. All Sindalki were like that.

I looked at the Sindalki lord sharply, but held my tongue.

Lord Aron spoke up firmly continuing his thoughts, which now seemed to be evolving into some kind of theory. "For our purposes, Jon Kirk, it does not mean whether your being some kind of a god is true or not. Of course we all know it is *not* true—you are certainly no god"—and Lord Aron even laughed out loud at the very ridiculousness of the premise and some others joined in his amusement at my expense. That made me feel better. Then he continued, "but the entity may believe it to be true. If so, that is all that matters to us now in dealing with it. And if this Kin-Ty-Roo believes this strange form of logic—and if only a god can slay another god—then you may be able to…"

"What? I am no god. I am a simple fighting man. I have reluctantly accepted the role of your emperor, to lead you all the best I am able and to keep our empire together, which I agree is necessary, but this is something very much out of my realm of experience, and I have no desire to…"

"Have a care my husband," Sirah quickly told me in a soft voice, her hand upon my arm in a light restraining gesture. "These are all friends here who mean you well. They do not mean you any harm."

I quieted down, looked at her and nodded, knowing she was correct. I cooled off a bit then. I had always considered myself a godly man valuing the goodly virtues as most fighting men and military people do—though I was never a formal church-going man back on Earth. However, this god thing bothered me immensely as I was a student of history, and knowledgeable about some of its darkest corners. It smacked to me of the arrogance and brutality of Ancient Rome with monsters like Caligula; the Pharaohs of long ago Egypt; or even Imperial Japan and its god emperor during World War II. I hated all that pretense of human leaders who proclaimed godhood or divinity. I did not want to go down that road. I would resist all efforts by the people of Ares, and of the empire overall, to push me in that direction. It was blasphemous and I would have none of it!

"Jon Kirk", Zaor now spoke to me carefully, as my best friend on Ares, who I respected above all other men. "If this entity believes it is a god—and that only another god can slay it—and if it believes you to be a god—then perhaps you *can* slay it? In fact, maybe *only* you can slay it?"

"What Lord Zaor says may be true," Lord Kneth spoke up firmly.

"I also agree," Aron The Eldest added with confidence. "The logic is there, not any logic that works in our normal reality, but it is a form of logic that may work in the reality of the entity. And that is the only logic that seems to matter now."

"Then it is the logic of a mad man-- or a man being!" I stated boldly.

"If the entity is a god of some kind, it may indeed be mad, Jon Kirk," Zaor added in a terse voice.

"Great! Now we have to defeat a mad god?"

Zaor allowed a dour grin, nodded, "Perhaps, but what has been said here now may be no less a form of logic for the entity, Jon Kirk."

I shook my head, "I do not know."

"None of us know about any of this for certain, Jon Kirk," Sahnjor now spoke up for the first time. He had quietly followed all the talk and gone over the logic and suppositions that had been put forth. "You may be able to slay it, Jon Kirk. In fact, you may be the only one who can do it, as Zaor has stated. You may have been close to killing it when you were inside the entity at the Place of Meaning. Your sword cut deep into the insides of it…."

"It was just the floor of the place," I added softly, but I did not believe my own words. I knew the damage I had inflicted upon the thing had been severe.

"That was not any mere flooring, it was a part of the entity that is most sensitive to its existence," the venerable Keven sage Lord Aron stated with certainty. "Jon Kirk, your sword cuts into that surface rendered the entity much pain and injury. Injury enough for us to place it in a compound stasis field through our mind master talents. Now locked in stasis it may be planning to fight against the god that hurt it—the human god that for the first time ever in its long eternal existence had given it an injury and damage—the being who proved to it that it is a god—the god Jon Kirk!"

"Don't call me that!" I shouted in anger.

"The entity, Jon Kirk, remember it only matters what the entity believes to be true—not us—not even *you*," Zaor reminded me.

"So now I guess I am some kind of entity too?" I growled in anger.

"Words, Jon Kirk, they are just words, and nothing to be overly concerned about," Aron The Eldest consoled me with his wisdom and serene calm. "As I told you once before when you were proclaimed Emperor of the Known Universe—it was for the good of all the people here and for their worlds that it should be made so—but the words are just words, my friend. The title is just a title, just words, a name, nothing more. No one will ever call you a god, rest assured. No one on Ares would ever be so blasphemous as to believe that conceit, but if this entity believes what it believes about itself—and it believes you to be a god as well—then so be it! Allow the entity to have its mad delusions about you. That will weaken it and may make it possible for you to defeat it. That is, after all, what we all want, Jon Kirk."

"I know, but I will certainly not become any kind of god!" I shouted still angry at the very thought.

"Of course not," Lord Aron replied firmly. "All here know that only *too* well."

I looked at Lord Aron carefully. I saw a hint of a smile cross his lips. Had he just made a joke at my expense? Then I heard a few laughs from those throughout the room.

Gorm seemed to think the statement positively funny and pounded the table with his massive fists in fits of laughing stitches. I looked at him, and then I laughed too, and the tension I felt inside me subsided. These were my friends, they would never do me wrong. I trusted them all and they had proven that trust to me a dozen times over. Sirah had been right and I had been foolish.

"A god? Most certainly not, my husband," Sirah added with a lovely smile as she kissed my lips, and I just laughed at the very thought of it all then, knowing she was putting me on in her own way and I for once saw the humor in the situation.

I nodded to Sirah, "My beloved, thank you."

"Jon Kirk, are all Earth men so silly? No one on Ares would ever believe you to be a god—any type of god—and certainly not me! I know you only too well, you see. You are just a man, only a man—but a good man, and maybe even a great man. That is far enough. However, you are still our emperor, so as you always say, you must 'do your duty.'"

I shook my head at her touching words but she just laughed joyfully, she was putting me on again and I laughed now along with her as the tension left me. "Yeah, emperor. Emperor of Ares and the Known Universe."

"And do not forget the Greens also," she added with a sly grin. "Especially *this* Green, my husband."

"Of course, how can I ever forget the Greens, I am married to the loveliest and most hard-headed of them all," I said with a slight smile.

"And never forget it, Jon Kirk!" Sirah told me offering me a slight wink. I had taught her the art of the wink and she liked it and used it well now.

I smiled back at her, she looked so lovely sitting there in her regal white dress, her green-hued skin glowing softly, her hair bright and flaming red like the fire red sun of Ares, her eyes sparkling with keen intelligence and her warm moist lips luscious and just waiting for my kisses. I took a needed deep breathe, for I was momentarily struck breathless by her sheer beauty. I kissed her then, hard and fast.

My wonderful husband..." she whispered in a husky voice. I nodded and smiled as I released her.

Sirah and I relaxed, the room grew quiet.

"All right now, so this entity believes itself to be a god, and it believes me to be a god as well. Then if only a god can kill another god, then now what?" I asked those around the table.

"My Lord, you have to understand we are discussing only what the entity believes to be true—not what is *actually* true," Sahn-jor spoke up with calm deliberation putting the entire conversation into perspective. "I make the distinction, but it is an important one, perhaps even crucial to our victory. This entity is apparently immortal, but it can be killed—but only by another god. It believes you to be another god. Therefore it believes that you can kill it. That seems to indicate that it will accept death at your hands, Jon Kirk. Do you realize what that means?"

I nodded, I think I now understood the difference behind all this god talk but it still rankled. "So what do I do about it, challenge it to a duel? Swords, or death ray weapons?"

"Not quite so simple, I am afraid, but perhaps there is no need to make it so personal as well," Lord Kneth chimed in. "You are the emperor of the Known Universe, your warships can surround the Kin-Ty-Roo and destroy it. You need but give the command. The fleet will do the work under your order and the entity will be killed under your order. That may be all that is required."

"It could be killed by our fleet whether I am thought to be a god or not," I advised carefully.

"Perhaps—or perhaps not," Lord Kneth added with a grim look. "However, I would not risk our fleet and crews without the added sanction of your so-called divinity. We do not know the thought process of this thing. Whatever its thought process may be, we can be assured that it is totally alien to our own way of thinking. That said, things must be done according to its rules—not ours. Perhaps it would resist the fleet if sent without your sanction—and it would most certainly know if this was so. And it might even bring in its own fleet to counter our own. That could mean the utter destruction of our fleet and crews. Their ships outnumber us ten to one. It could do this easily, I am afraid. However, I believe we are blessed in this matter, Jon Kirk. For if it did not believe you to be a god, things might be far worse for us all."

I nodded, thinking it through. I now saw the logic of his words and the possibilities of the situation. It seemed to be crazy logic to me, but a form of logic nonetheless. I did not like it, but if there was a chance this would work then I would take it!

"There is something else," Lord Kneth added in a thoughtful voice that got everyone's attention. "There seems to be some evidence that the entity may be, in fact, actually *seeking* its own death."

This was something new to me that I had not heard before.

"Exactly what do you mean by that?" I quickly asked Lord Kneth.

There was no answer from Lord Kneth or anyone else.

Was this mad alien entity suicidal as well?

I looked at the many people seated around that vast table in that huge room. "Are you telling me that the entity actually *wants* to die? That it seeks death? It seems incredible to me but that is what some of you seem to be hinting at. And if you are correct, then there must be some evidence for this, and a reason for it."

Lord Kneth looked grim and replied sternly, "There is. The fleet of the entity is nowhere to be found in Known Space. Is this fleet in hiding? It seems inconceivable that such a massive fleet would be hiding at this crucial time. Why hide? What could it possibly fear? Or has it simply been sent away? That seems more plausible. So then, why has the entity sent away its very large and powerful fleet? Again I ask, if so, why? Why would the many warships of the Enemy Empire leave their 'god' unattended? Why leave their master held prisoner by us in stasis, where it is also open to our attack and possible destruction? What is going on here? I can only assume that it was done on purpose."

I nodded, it certainly made some kind of sense. I said, "I thought this thing existed to feed, but now it is *not* feeding and some of you believe that this seemingly immortal god is seeking its own death. It does not make any sense to me. Why? I am afraid I do not understand any of this."

I looked at my friends and advisors, ministers and other empire leaders for some clarification. The faces that looked back at me were mostly blank, and some were simply terrified, for these were matters far outside of their experience and knowledge.

Aron The Eldest spoke up finally, "We do not know, My Emperor. We do not know anything for certain about this alien entity."

Suddenly Crooch spoke up once again, "Jon Kirk, I know one thing for certain, you must send the fleet and destroy the Kin-Ty-Roo. It must be destroyed soon, and you are the only one who can give the order for this to be done."

Many in that chamber echoed Crooch's words. My world was truly upside down when such a reptile as this terrible former villain had become a part of my inner circle, and his advice was now agreed to by most of the leaders of the empire—including in some manner, myself. It was truly a strange turn of events.

CHAPTER 11

The Turning Point

"Jon Kirk?" Zaor asked me later when we were standing alone outside the Great Hall, "What is your problem? Why do you hesitate? I can lead the fleet, or Admiral Quarto-Zar can lead it, if you like—under your orders of course. All you need do is give us the word. Then we can vaporize this Kin-Ty-Roo once and for all and be rid of it."

"My friend, I am aware what is the right course here, the proper decision. In any case it will be one we will all have to live with—or die with from then on—once my decision has been made and carried out."

"Of course, I realize that, but why do you hesitate? This is most unlike you. You are a man of action, as am I. I understand that events have taken a strange turn. I never thought I would be in agreement with a scoundrel and traitor like that *chavas* Crooch—even though he did save your life—but believe me no one is more surprised to find that I am in agreement with him in this action than I am—as are so are many of your closest and most trusted ministers and advisors."

I sighed, shaking my head, "I know that, Zaor, but I find myself contemplating the time travel option once again. If we can send this thing far back in time, while it is still enclosed as a prisoner in the stasis field, that may be something that could solve all our problems once and for all. Ras-noor is working on the possibilities of it now."

"Ah, yes, Ras-noor, he is a most capable fellow, but science will not get us out of this problem now, Jon Kirk, only cold hard steel and powerful death ray weapons will get the job done."

I nodded, "Perhaps you are right, my friend. I will think upon it."

"Do not think upon it too long, My Emperor," Zaor spoke to me using a serious tone with my formal title, letting me know that while we were friends, I was still the leader of this empire—and as so, I was expected to lead.

Of course I thought that was exactly what I was doing, trying my best to make the correct decision with limited facts—which is the hardest part of being a leader. It was proving a thankless job, and yet, there was no one else who could do it, but myself. I had taken on the leadership role and now it was up to me to lead us to victory.

I walked away from Zaor with many thoughts weighing heavily upon my mind. On the way to my personal chambers I met Aron The Eldest. The wise old Keven mind master seemed in deep thought as he approached me. He looked troubled, cautious.

"What is it?" I asked, for I could see that something was bothering him.

"Jon Kirk, there is much to all this that does not seem to make sense to me," he told me carefully, in a most serious tone.

"You're telling me!" I suddenly laughed out loud, for not much about all this made sense to me either and I openly admitted it.

Lord Aron only frowned, he did not see the humor, he was not joking, and I thought better of taking his concerns too lightly.

"All right, what is it, my friend?" I asked carefully.

"I am being most serious, My Emperor. Ever since you came back from Lord Doom's warship in your meeting and alliance with Crooch, we have discovered much about this Kin-Ty-Roo, but I wonder how much of it is true. Or accurate. I have my suspicions."

I gave Lord Aron a sharp look. I was not in the mood to hear negative words about Crooch just then, for he had saved my life and I felt I owed him a certain measure of loyalty and respect. Nevertheless, Lord Aron's words troubled me, for if he felt something was wrong here—if he felt that we were being somehow tricked or trapped—I definitely wanted to know about it.

I looked at Lord Aron closely, "Crooch freed me from Doom's ship and then helped to save my life. He has shown nothing but loyalty since that moment."

"True," Lord Aron stated, unmoving, apparently unimpressed by my words. I did not blame him for that, for Crooch had a most vile history.

"So there is more? All right, Aron, I understand, you formed a mind meld and entered Crooch's mind going down into the lowest depths, and saw all that was there. A putrid pit I am sure. You told me there was no treachery in him now, only fear of the entity and his strong belief that it must be destroyed as soon as possible." I stated the facts as we both knew them up to that point in time.

"That is true, Jon Kirk."

I looked hard at Lord Aron, "So then what is bothering you?"

"I do not know. Perhaps it is just the sense of all this."

"The *sense* of it? Ah, you are not being clear but I think I see it now. Is it because this does not seem to add up? It does not seem to contain that stern logic that you Kevens are so fond of?" I asked him, for I had a niggling fear of that myself. Sometimes logic could seem most, illogical.

Lord Aron surprised me by his next statement. "No, not quite. In fact, what really bothers me, is that everything we know regarding the entity seems to add up only too well. It was mentioned earlier that it seemed as if the entity wanted you to destroy it."

I looked at Lord Aron closely now, speaking to him most carefully, "Well, yes, I may have aid that, as did some others in the war council, including yourself, I seem to remember, but it was just a wild thought that came up because of the frustration we all felt at the time. I did not take it seriously. I do not believe others did as well. You know, I was angry over all that talk of me being spoken of as some kind of a god. I find that insulting and…most ungodly."

"As do I, My Emperor, but I have a nagging fear that we may have inadvertently struck true with that wild remark."

"How so?" I asked with growing concern now. What was he up to?

Lord Aron shrugged, "I do not know for certain. I have no evidence to prove my feelings on this matter. And at this point they are only feelings with no real substance to them—which also disturbs me. I only know that more and more of your inner circle now stand firmly behind Crooch and Zaor's plan to destroy the entity."

"Well, that is certainly logical," I told the Keven with a wry grin. "Zaor is a fighting man and I fully understand his marital feelings in this matter—I have them myself and were I not emperor…"

"But you are emperor, Jon Kirk."

"All right, I understand that duty and accept it, which I know means that I must think more far a field and see the bigger picture. I do understand that. But destruction of the entity is a popular and necessary reaction to the threat it poses to us. As for Crooch, I owe him a debt for his deeds—and I understand his fear of the entity only too well. Remember, I was inside that creature at the Place of Meaning not very long ago. The thought of it still causes me to break out in a cold sweat."

Lord Aron shrugged, seemingly not very impressed by my words, "I have spoken about this with Lord Kneth and he and I would plead with you to act more cautiously here, Jon Kirk. There is some form of treachery afoot. The minds of men seem to be subtly changing in their orientation, in their very thoughts. The Sindalki lord and I believe we have noticed such changes of thought."

"Changes? In what way?" I asked alarmed now by his words. I knew Lord Aron and Lord Kneth were the two greatest mind masters we had among us, they were sensitive to all manner of mental forces—most of which I did not understand. Was this, in fact, some kind of new trap set for us by our enemy?

"More and more of your loyal ministers and advisors, generals and leaders of the empire seem to be supporting the call for immediate destruction of the entity by your war fleet," Lord Aron told me simply.

I nodded, well that seemed logical to me. I allowed a nervous grin, this did not seem to be much out of the usual.

I said, "I expect as much, my friend. Why are you so alarmed? It is only natural that eventually a consensus will form, and that it would form on the side of the destruction of the entity."

"Of course, I realize that may be true, as you do, but I do not like it," he told me with a nervous look in his old eyes. "I do not like it— if that is what the entity wants!"

"What it *wants*?" I asked carefully curious, with growing alarm.

"Yes, what it *wants*," Aron repeated firmly.

I froze, looked at him closely, then nodded, "I will take it under advisement, my friend."

"I am not certain on this mode of thought, Jon Kirk, but it could be possible that our minds are being manipulated or tampered with. Or it may just be the confusion and stress placed upon an old man from Kev who has seen too much evil in his overly long life," Lord Aron stated with a forced grin.

"Do not worry, it will work out, I am sure," I told him as I placed my hand on his shoulder in a brotherly gesture of support.

"Of course, My Emperor."

I left him there in the hallway and walked the short distance to my private apartments with a hundred thoughts colliding inside my mind. I passed alert guards, my loyal Black Dragons posted at every intersection in every corridor throughout the Imperial Palace. All looked as it should be. The warriors were alert and on guard.

I entered my private apartments and smiled at the sight of my beloved Sirah. She had been waiting for me. We hugged and kissed warmly.

"These are troubling times, my love," she told me, sensing my mood.

"Yes, and a time of difficult decisions."

"Then allow me to help you."

"Please do," I stated holding her tightly in my arms.

"Send in the fleet," she said simply.

I smiled, looking deeply into her lovely sparkling eyes, "Are you serious?"

"Yes, it is the only way," she replied in a husky tone. "Kill the entity and Ares will be safe. We will all be safe."

"I only wish I could be certain that would be true. Things may not be so simple. Do you not think such an action might be precisely what the entity might want us to do?"

"No, how can that be?" she asked me, showing a strange concern by my words which now surprised me.

"Well, I say that because we know it has moved off its fleet, it has not attacked us, it has left itself open to attack by our own fleet. It has also ceased feeding. Something is going on. Something seems to be going wrong here."

"Nothing seems wrong here, my love, but I do not know all the answers, Jon Kirk. Perhaps you should seek further clarification from Lord Kneth? He is most wise in these matters."

I nodded, I told her I would do so and then left the chambers.

CHAPTER 12

The Thinking

I went immediately to Lord Kneth's quarters. My aim was to find out what the Sindalki lord could tell me about what might be going on among my people being influenced by the enemy. I thought it wise at this point to have Tor-nul and four of my Black Dragons bodyguard accompany me wherever I went, even in the palace. You could never tell what mischief was brewing these days, and I knew the palace was becoming a hotbed for mystery and, even perhaps, treachery. I also had Tor-nul station a dozen Black Dragons at my apartments in the palace to protect the Empress and my son, Alun. If anything were to happen to them I would never forgive myself. Tor-nul and his men were relentlessly efficient and could be most deadly when necessary. I felt better with them close at hand and watching on high alert.

I found Lord Kneth alone in his chamber and he bid me enter his rooms as if he expected me. I was curious by his manner. I left Tor-nul and his men outside stationed in the outer hallway for I wanted to speak to the Sinsalki lord alone.

"My Lord Kneth," I said, exchanging formal greetings with him as he showed me into his private quarters. I had never been there before and wondered how a Sindalki lord lived.

"My Emperor. What brings you here to my most humble rooms?" he replied to me with a the usual stoic look upon his face. He was always such a serious individual.

I took a quick look around at Lord Kneth's lavish suite of rooms there in the palace of Tarcos. They were anything but humble, in fact extravagant would be more like the word for it, but I restrained a wry grin or comment at his obvious enjoyment of excess luxury and got down to the serious business at hand.

"I was speaking to Lord Aron a short time ago, and he told me you and he had a certain feeling about the coming events—a feeling that perhaps they did not ring so true. Can you explain that?"

"Lord Aron said that to you, My Lord? Truly? I can not understand why. I have always been most open and honest in my thoughts and quite consistent in my advice to you."

I nodded, acknowledging the truth of his words. "Of course, Lord Kneth, and I duly appreciate it. But Lord Aron told me you and he felt there was some situation, or some trouble—something going on behind the scenes that I should be alert too. Nothing definite yet, just a feeling he told me he felt. He also said you were concerned about the fleet attacking the entity."

Lord Kneth looked up at me with genuine surprise then, "I do not understand, My Emperor. I have always supported the plan to have our fleet destroy the Kin-Ty-Roo."

I looked at the Sindalki lord closely trying to hide my shock and surprise, but kept my true feelings firmly under control for now. His words shook me and shocked me, but I tried not to show any feelings, for I knew his words were not true.

I looked at Lord Kneth most carefully. Exactly what was he telling me? Was he being serious? Or was he outright lying? There was something definitely wrong here. I could feel it, and it was more than just an inkling now.

The Sindalki lord had *never* held this view and it was well known by me and others, but he seemed quite serious about it now. How? Why? What had so firmly changed in his mind?

I decided to lightly press him upon the matter. "I have to admit I am a bit confused. I do not believe that is what you told me only a few short hours ago at the war council, My Lord."

"No, I am sorry but that can not be correct, My Emperor," he said in all seriousness. His appearance of total honesty did not waver. I looked at him closely and saw no sign of deception. Only honest truth. That was even more perplexing. He totally believed what he was telling me. That only raised more questions within me that must be answered.

I was astounded by hearing these words and they set me aback for a moment. I looked carefully at Lord Kneth, and the more I looked at him, the more the hairs upon the back of my neck stood up in sudden fear and horror. This was outright wrong! This was not true at all! Something was very out of place here!

Had the Kin-Ty-Roo worked its mind spells or magic upon Lord Kneth? Was the Sindalki no longer trustworthy—or had he even become an agent of my enemy now? If so, how many others in the palace had had their minds altered or interfered with the same way? I knew now that the strange and sudden change of mind of many of those closest to me might be due to some other reason than a simple and natural change in their personal opinion based on the facts. That put a terrible chill within me. If what I feared was happening, then who could I trust?

Zaor, my best friend, and my beloved Sirah, both had recently changed their views concerning an attack upon the entity—or at least Sirah definitely had changed her view on the matter. She was now strongly for the attack. Much like Crooch, I thought. That got me thinking down a road I did not want to consider going down. Was Sirah under some mind control or influence by the alien entity? The very thought horrified me and indicated deadly danger for us all if such a thing was possible.

I looked again at the Sindalki who stood before me. Was Lord Kneth now also under some mind spell? If so, how many others were so controlled, and how did I break the spell of this control? I could not afford to lose the support of one so important as Lord Kneth and any of the others. Who to trust?

I decided that if what I feared was happening, if it was indeed really happening, then a more sly tack was needed here. I would not confront the Sindalki outright. I would play along with him as if I was in agreement with his opinion.

"It seems, Lord Kneth, perhaps I made some error. Allow me to be clear on this matter. So, you do not believe that the Kin-Ty-Roo is influencing you or anyone else here in the palace in any way? And you have come to your decision independently and of your own volition that the fleet should be sent to destroy the alien entity?"

"Jon Kirk, My Emperor, my friend, I am sure my mind is not under any foreign influence, I assure you. That simply can not happen," — then he looked at me closely—"however I can not speak for anyone else here, of course."

"Of course," I responded softly.

The Sindalki continued, "And as for the attack on the entity, you know only too well that I was always for it, ever since the beginning."

I looked hard at Lord Kneth, his thoughts, words, demeanor, all seemed genuine. He was not lying. He was telling me the truth—*as far as he believed it to be the truth*—but it was not at all what I remembered hearing him tell me just a short time ago.

I felt a cold chill run up my back. There was something very wrong here. I now had to accept the fact that somehow members of my inner circle had been infiltrated by some foreign influence. I wondered if the Kin-Ty-Roo was still even held in stasis any longer—perhaps it had escaped? Or perhaps even from within stasis it was able to use its vast mind control powers against us? It was a truly terrifying prospect that I had not anticipated and did not know how to fight against.

Then a thought even worse than this entered my mind. Could these thoughts be influenced only inside my own mind? Were my very thoughts being manipulated or tampered with? I feared that might be the case, but only for a dire dark moment did I consider the idea, then I deftly discarded it. No, that could not be correct, in fact I seemed immune somehow from all outside mind manipulation. I knew the enemy powers, whatever they were, did not seem to have any control or influence over me at all—but they certainly seemed to do so to some of those around me. It was uncanny. Perhaps my seeming immunity was because I was an Earthman and not of Ares? I am an outworlder. A stranger here. Whatever the reason, and whatever was going on now, I knew I needed to speak immediately to Aron the Eldest upon the matter. He was the one mind master here that I could trust and whose knowledge might be able to help me. Or so I hoped.

* * * *

I found Lord Aron with the other Kevens discussing some mind meld topics in heated argument. That in itself seemed most unusual. Kevens did not argue.

"Lord Aron, I need to speak with you a moment," I asked the Keven wise man interrupting his group of mind masters and their discussion.

"Yes, My Emperor," he replied in a friendly enough tone, and we walked off to be alone. Tor-nul and my Black Dragons had followed me and still stood guard ever ready, but at a respectful distance and well out of earshot.

"I want to ask you something. I had the most extraordinary conversation with Lord Kneth moments ago. Are you aware that he is now in full support of the fleet attacking the entity? He seems to have no reservations about this at all now."

"No, I was not aware of that, but that is certainly good to hear," Lord Aron stated in obvious relief and sincerity.

Now I really had a creepy feeling. I did an immediate double-take upon hearing these words from my friend. I looked at the Keven carefully with a most dubious and stern gaze trying to figure out what I had just heard from his own lips. Something seemed wrong here as well now. This was not at all what Lord Aron had told me barely hours ago when we had spoken upon this very topic.

Lord Aron had also mentioned to me then that he had feared the possibility of a foreign influence effecting the minds of some of our people. That seemed to be the case now for certain and I knew I had to proceed with great care as my key people seemed to be changing their opinions most suspiciously. Under what influence was this change of thought being done? And it caused me to have the thought, what other ideas where being fed into their minds? Now who could I trust? Could I even trust myself?

"Lord Aron, I have to tell you quite candidly, that is not what you told me only a few hours ago," I stated, looking at him intently to gauge his reaction to my words. He appeared calm, unaffected, the usual kind and thoughtful Keven mind master I had always known. But something was subtly different about him now. Something was not quite right here. I grew nervous and cautious. I knew I had to tread lightly on what I said to him now.

He smiled at me warmly, "Of course, Jon Kirk, that may be true, but I have since changed my view upon the matter. My thoughts and my reaction has evolved. It is the logical reaction. The entity is incredibly dangerous, hence it must be destroyed."

"So you have changed your mind upon the matter based upon the logic and facts of the situation?"

"Yes, of course, that is the only credible reason."

I looked at him carefully, nodded, "All right, fair enough."

"And I ask you to heed my consul on the matter now and come to agreement with me on this matter as well and act quickly."

"Of course, and I will do so soon," I replied carefully, thoughtfully, a dubious look furrowing my brow, but I hid it in an attempt not to raise his suspicions. I tried to hide my true thoughts from his mind master talents, and Lord Aron being the honorable man that he was, did not try to read them.

"That is good to hear, My Emperor."

"When we last spoke you mentioned to me the possibility that some of our people might have their thoughts come under the influence of the entity. Have you detected who those people might be?"

Aron The Eldest looked at me carefully, thoughtfully, "I recall the conversation, Jon Kirk, but I have been unable to discover any foreign intrusion into the thoughts or actions of any of our people. We were in the process of building a new mind meld to examine the people here in the palace when an argument broke out among a small group of my people."

"The Kevens are in argument? I thought you were always in harmony?" I asked allowing my curious tone to show, but masking my outright sudden surprise at hearing this troubling news.

"So it is, in the usual manner of doing these things, but that seems to have changed now for some unaccountable reason," Lord Aron said rather sadly.

"Well, then what is the reason for this argument?" I asked, still curious, insistent to hear his explanation.

"Nothing serious, I assure you, My Lord. Many of us have changed our minds and are in full agreement and support the immediate attack by the fleet upon the entity. We want it to happen right away. The destruction of the entity must be paramount in our action. A few hard-headed younger fellows remain obstinate against such an action."

"And these others?"

"They are still obstinate and refuse to come to agreement with us."

"I see, and who are these obstinate fellows?"

"They are over there, the four moody Elders talking alone among themselves by the far wall. They are lesser and younger mind masters newly installed by me as Elders. I am always seeking to increase our ranks. They have great potential and talent but seem to be…confused. They will come around, I am sure."

I left Lord Aron and went over to the four Keven elders.

"My Emperor!" all four stated as one and then bowed.

I nodded to them, then said, "Lord Aron tells me you are having an argument and you do not believe the fleet attacking the entity to be a good idea."

They were silent for a long and rather cautious moment, which told me much, each one looking at the other. They had not expected my blunt question or how to properly reply to it.

"Yes, My Emperor," the boldest of the fellows said coming forward from the group. He was named Kon, a man who seemed to be the leader of these fellows. They were certainly newer and younger Elders, all had black or green hair, rather than white hair, or being entirely bald as were most Keven Elders. They were obviously younger men, newly installed as mind masters by Lord Aron himself, who was always seeking to expand the members in their ranks in order to increase their total mind powers.

Something was up here and I was determined to get to the bottom of it—but I knew I had to do so carefully.

"So what is going on here, Lord Kon?" I asked the leader of the four uncooperative Kevens. Non cooperation was a most un-Keven way for them to be.

"We do not know, Jon Kirk. We have noted some peculiarities in the thoughts of many of the higher level people in power here in the palace. We have not the mind master talents yet to determine exactly what is happening, but we feel there seems to be something that may not be quite *true* here."

"Indeed, and I assume you have brought this to the attention of Lord Aron?"

"Of course," Kon stated firmly, the other three nodded rapt agreement.

"And what was his reaction?"

"Most interesting. He told me that we were in error, My Emperor, and that we were being uncooperative. It is most unlike him to take that kind of reaction to the question we posed, which could be a serious threat to us all. I feel that something is wrong," Kon said now allowing dark concern to show upon his face.

"Indeed, you may be right," I admitted in a low tone to him and his fellows so that only they could hear my words.

Lord Kon looked at me carefully and then sighed in deep relief at my agreement with him, thankfully. He whispered softly, "My Emperor, so you feel it as well?"

"I feel that something unusual is happening here, Lord Kon. I want you and your men to leave here at once and report to Ras-noor immediately. Perhaps you can be of help to him."

The four Kevens saluted as one and were soon gone.

Lord Aron came over to me soon afterwards. My good friend, my great ally, and yet now like so many others he seemed to have fallen under a cloud of suspicion. I did not know who to trust now, or if I could even trust him and Lord Kneth. If that was true I was in a dire predicament. In truth, at this point, I even doubted to trust myself.

I looked at Lord Aron carefully. He seemed to be the same wise gentle old mind master I had known and respected for so long. He was truly a great man and a friend, and he was a key part of our leadership and a valued member of my inner circle—but I knew something was wrong about him now. Something did not add up. He seemed to be under some outside influence—as were many others apparently.

"Kon and his three companions?" Lord Aron asked me curiously.

"Obviously they are troublemakers," I stated calmly, giving him a look that told him I was annoyed with Kon and his fellows and I did not approve of them. "I sent them away. I do not want them to interfere with the valuable work you are doing here. I am sure you will not miss them."

"No, they are not needed here, their thoughts disrupt us. Thank you, Jon Kirk, that is most wise, but I would place a watch upon them if I were you."

"Good advice. I will do so."

"I do not think they are to be trusted," Lord Aron added, which was most unusual for him to be so suspicious. This was not quite the Lord Aron I knew.

"I will have them watched. Now you continue with your work here," I told the Keven leader and then left him. Thoughts of him and others in the palace being compromised now weighted heavily upon me.

I met up with Tor-nul and my Black Dragons bodyguard outside Lord Aron's room. "Tor-nul, we are going to need more men. More guards to be posted, eyes everywhere, there is treachery afoot."

Tor-nul looked worried, he knew that I never had guards posted throughout the palace, or accompanying my person, so he was sure something was up even before I admitted it to him. "What do you want me to do, Jon Kirk?"

"For now, just post your guards on everyone in the palace, quietly, unobtrusively, tell them it is for their own safety, and have General Zaor sent to me right away."

CHAPTER 13

The Reason Is Made Clear

"Zaor, you and Tor-nul may be the only members of my inner circle here in the palace who I can now trust," I told the two warriors confidentially. We were in a private chamber I used for meetings with small groups. It was just the three of us there and I saw their faces grow grim at my words. I continued voicing my concerns, getting it all out in the open now, "I fear the entity has somehow affected some control or influence over the thoughts of many of my key advisors and ministers."

"How so? And to what end?" Zaor asked me sharply concerned.

"The aim seems to be to push me into making a precipitous decision. The decision of authorizing a full scale attack by our fleet upon the alien entity," I told him, laying out the truth of my thoughts now to him, and to Tor-nul, the commander of my elite bodyguard.

Zaor looked at me wryly and just shook his head in evident confusion, "But, Jon Kirk, I advise the exact same action."

"And I as well," Tor-nul added firmly with a shake of his head.

"Do you think that Tor-nul and I have been somehow…?" Zaor asked tensely.

I shook my head negatively, looking at my two good friends and trusted warriors warmly, "Not you two, I am sure, for I know there is no foreign influence in your thoughts—I am sure of that. I trust you both. Your minds can not be interfered with in this manner because you are first, and above all, fighting men. Your thoughts are the clear natural thoughts of all true fighting men. That means much."

Zaor nodded and accepted this logic with a wry grin, saying, "Of course," as if it were the most natural thing in the world, and to him it was just that simple.

"I agree with the general, Jon Kirk," Tor-nul added confidently.

"I know you do, and I know that it is the result of your own free will and unfettered opinion, and that you are not under the control of any outside influence. It is not necessary with either of you to have your opinions altered. You already agree with the action to attack the entity and your opinion comes from your long military training and from the facts. With some of the others here, I am not so sure."

"If what you are telling us is true, then this is a serious problem, Jon Kirk. Who are these others?" Zaor asked carefully, curious that treason might now be in the wind.

I sighed resignedly, "Too many good people who are too close to us, my friends. Sahn-jor, Aron The Eldest, Lord Kneth, even my own lovely Sirah, your own sister," I said, though it pained me greatly to say it.

"Truly?" Zaor asked with deep concern.

"I believe so, I am sorry, my friend."

"It can not be, Jon Kirk," he refused to believe it.

"It is true. I am afraid that it is true, Zaor," I told him firmly.

"Then we are truly in deadly peril."

Tor-nul said nothing, but his eyes were wide with alert tension.

I looked at my two most noble warriors and best friends and asked them, "Yes we are in peril, but why is this happening? Think about it. Why this push to cause me to order an immediate attack upon the entity? What does it want? Does it want a fight? And why does it remain alone and unguarded in The Empty Quarter? Seemingly easy prey for us. Where is the Enemy Empire fleet? Where are all their many warships? They have a thousand warships! Why are they not on guard—or even attacking us? These are all questions I must have answered before I can make my decision upon this matter," I stated trying to put all the pieces of this complex puzzle together in my mind, and then voicing them before my two most rusted warriors. I knew I was missing many important valuable pieces for the solution of this most perplexing puzzle.

We were quiet and thoughtful for a long moment at this dire news, each of us mired in our own thoughts. I could see Zaor was disturbed that Sirah might be under some influence of the entity—I was so fearful of what it might mean.

Suddenly there was a knock to the door, and the senior guard of my Black Dragons posted in the outer hallway let in Ras-noor and the mind master Lord Kon, along with his three Keven companions.

They all walked into the room and took in the scene immediately. It was a small chamber, just the emperor and two warriors. Here I was, Emperor of the Greens, Emperor of all Ares, Emperor of the Known Universe of all the damn things—a man who was now even thought to be a god of some kind by some crazy alien entity who also thought itself to be a god—and here I was meeting in secret in some small nondescript room like some sinister plotter or spy. Nothing could be more bizarre.

"Now we are all here," I said, acknowledging each of the newcomers to enter the room and take a seat.

"Now we are all here?" Lord Kon asked concerned.

"Here for what, My Emperor?" Ras-noor asked guardedly suspicious.

Now Ras-noor, Kon and his three fellows nervously and carefully joined Zaor, Tor-nul and myself in secluded secrecy. The chamber door was closed and secured.

"What is this?" Ras-nor asked allowing his suspicion to show.

"This is a meeting of all those in the empire that I feel I can trust," I stated simply with a grim look into the face of each man there.

There was tense silence from each man as the full import of my words sank into their thoughts. I saw some of them nod their heads gravely in agreement.

Ras-noor allowed a grim look upon his old weathered green face, "Yes, I for one have observed some rather strange changes of thought over the last day or two. Lord Kon and his fellows have noted likewise and have just told me of their thoughts upon this matter. I am most appreciative you sent him and his fellow Kevens to me, for otherwise I might have thought my lone suspicions to be odd and not quite sane. I feared that some form of madness might be upon me. It now appears we all have these similar suspicions, and that they may be valid, Jon Kirk."

"Yes," I admitted to them firmly.

"So what do we do about it?" Zaor asked boldly, ready for action as always.

I asked the scientist, "Ras-noor, is the entity still held in stasis? Is it still secure?"

"Yes, My Emperor, it is—as far as we can tell. Yet, who can truly be sure of anything concerning such a creature."

"But it appears to be secure for now?" I prompted.

"Yes, it seems to be."

"Good, then I need to know if it is possible that it can exert control or influence on minds here through the stasis field?" I continued with a daunting question that I feared the answer to.

Ras-noor didn't even have to think that one over for long, he confidently replied, "Yes, in fact it appears that it is doing that now."

I nodded grimly, expecting as much. It was a terrifying realization. This was a fine pickle to be in. I had to think about what was going on here now and come up with a way to meet this threat and neutralize it. However, first I had to come up with the right questions to ask, before I could get the correct answers. What exactly were we dealing with here?

"Tell me, what do you believe to be the aim of this entity?" I asked those around me in that small group of trusted men.

Zaor shrugged, replied simply, "To feed, to eat, to control and conquer."

"But it is doing none of that now. Not at all, really," I said looking over to my chief scientist.

Ras-noor was silent, thinking, shaking his head.

"Well?" I promoted him.

"I have thought much upon what was spoken of in the palace war council hours ago. This idea that the entity is a god and that it sees you as a god as well, Jon Kirk. If that logic holds true, and if it can only be killed by another god, then it seems that for some reason it wants you to kill it. It may even be seeking you out to kill it, Jon Kirk!"

We all looked askance at Ras-noor but I saw Lord Kon and even Zaor nod their heads in agreement to his words. I was not so sure. It seemed incredible to me—even preposterous. Was this some insane so-called god? Or some suicidal alien entity?

"Seeking me out?" I asked those around me perplexed.

"Yes, Jon Kirk," Ras-noor replied with sure confidence and a steady gaze.

"But why? For what purpose?" I asked dumbfounded. "Why would an all-powerful alien being want to seek its own destruction? Is it insane? Suicidal?"

"Who knows, but for some reason it seems that it seeks its own death, but it can only be killed by another god," Zaor stated simply.

"Yes, but I am certainly no god!" I said angered once again by the very thought.

"No, but it *believes* you to be a god, and that is all that matters," Ras-noor stated with a firm determined voice. "I am not positive of this, but it apparently wants you to kill it. It may even be seeking you out, to perform the killing. There must be some reason behind this, but it evades me. Why it seeks this action, I have no idea."

"So it has been seeking me? But why me?" I asked with a confused look to my face. "I am nothing, certainly no one special."

"Jon Kirk, my friend," Zaor stated firmly, even boldly, "you surely underestimate yourself. Your great fighting abilities and your many incredible victories have become legend. You came to Ares not long ago with nothing and rose to free the Greens from the slavery of the hated Winged-men; you then formed the Green Empire of the six liberated cities; you next fought and defeated the invisible Blue Men from Vognar, and their Winged-men allies whose plan was to re-conquer Ares. Next you defeated the Secret Empire fleet of the Sindalki when it came to conquer Ares; then you fought the traitor Lord Doom and his fleet, and even killed Lord Doom himself. You then traveled far through the void of space to an area within the Kin-Ty-Roo itself to attack it and you were victorious in causing it pain and severe distress. Your attack upon it seems to have weakened it enough so that we could place it in a stasis prison. Your accomplishments are truly great—even legend! So to this entity, you *are* a god, and to its way of thinking, it was not in error in seeking you out."

I swallowed hard, Zaor's list of my accomplishments since I had first come to Ares was long and impressed even me. I had been through so much, yet what I held most dear now were not all the victories he had mentioned—as nice as they were and as much as they helped the people of Ares—but what was important to me was my beloved wife, Sirah, and our little son, Alun. They were what I fought for. They were the meaning of my life.

"But why?" I asked incredulous. "It makes no sense to me."

"No sense to you, My Emperor—or to any of us either, but it seems to be so, it surely makes sense to the entity," Ras-noor stated with a serious nod of his head.

"Who can say for sure why this is so, My Emperor," Zaor added. "It is an alien, and alien thoughts are most alien to our own. Unknown and maybe even unknowable."

Lord Kon spoke up then, "My companions and I believe that the entity seeks the release of death, but it must be for some very specific reason."

"Ah, yes, the release of death," Ras-noor continued thoughtfully. "Now when you put it in those terms…"

"What terms? What do you mean?" I demanded of the wily old scientist.

"Death is certainly a form of release—the release from life," Ras-noor told us carefully, "but release can also mean something else. It may lead to something more."

"What else? What more?" Tor-nul blurted in excited anticipation.

"Release can presage a new beginning, a great change, or a new birth—or perhaps a re-birth," Ras-noor stated with calm deliberation.

"Birth? Re-birth?" I said softly, thoughtfully, meaningfully, repeating the words.

I looked at the old scientist with deep concern now. What the hell did he mean? And then it came to me. The entity being found alone in The Empty Quarter of deep space, helpless, unprotected by its great fleet. The Enemy Empire fleet gone. Gone because it was not needed any longer? Gone where? Who knows. Sent away? Apparently sent away. Gone because it was no longer useful or needed. The entity was ready to seek the release of death according to its own sense of logic and truth. I told this to my small group of trusted conspirators.

"It needs you, Jon Kirk, to attain its goal. You are the key factor to it attaining its goal. Only a god can kill another god—as far as the entity's way of thinking goes. It seems to be seeking you out. Maybe there is some cosmic rational for this, some deeper meaning or law of science or magic from the place where it comes from—or maybe not?" Ras-noor tried to explain in mere words what was not meant to be spoken of in mere words. "Whatever it is, it is seeking to create a situation where you kill it. It wants the release of death and it needs you to be the one that causes that death. It wants to influence you—

through the members of your inner circle—to immediately order the fleet into action against it to kill it. Then it will be dead and receive the release that it seeks."

"Release of what?" I demanded in a low growl.

"I cannot say for certain, Jon Kirk, the entity is far too alien to be understood by mortal minds or our conventional standards," Ras-noor replied carefully.

I looked to Lord Kon and his three Keven companions. "Do you have any thoughts upon the matter? If so, I need to hear them now."

Lord Kon swallowed nervously, he was extremely serious, uncomfortable to be here and away from his Keven brothers, "My Emperor, I can not be certain on this at all, but I ask myself the question, what is the key imperative of all life? It is to eat, to feed—but why does it do that? It does that so that it can reproduce!"

I looked at Lord Kon unable to hold down my terror at what his words meant for us all. The implications were terrifying if true. Certainly that tangential thought had fleetingly entered my mind, as it had others, but it seemed incredulous that this might be the true final goal of the entity. Until this moment I had never actually seriously considered that it might be true. It seemed too fantastic to believe that it needed me to achieve its goal. Maybe too simple as well. If the entity was some kind of all-powerful god, why did it even need to reproduce? It was immortal, after all. Or was it? If it could be killed, then perhaps it was not as immortal as we—or as it—thought. It was certainly long-lived, and that might be the source of its god-like powers and even its thoughts of godhood. It could be hurt, I knew that now too. So perhaps it was not a god at all? I could not be sure, and all of this information and supposition was too much to accept all at once. Most confusing.

Ras-noor spoke up then, "If this is true, then it will be killed and die, and in doing so release the seeds—or whatever the related item may be—of hundreds, maybe even millions of smaller versions of itself into the Known Universe. They will infect all the great void of outer space all around us. Then they will begin to devour. Everything will be destroyed. No world, no people will be safe."

I felt a cold chill crawling up my spine at this dire prediction.

"So are you saying that it must be destroyed, or not?" Zaor asked curiously, confused. "And if what you say is true, isn't that exactly what this entity wants?"

Ras-noor and Lord Kon shook their heads violently, "No! Jon Kirk, Zaor, what we are saying is quite the opposite. We are saying that under no circumstances must the entity be destroyed. You can not send the fleet to destroy the Kin-Ty-Roo. We believe that to do so would cause the release of hundreds, thousands, or perhaps millions of similar monsters to devour all life throughout the universe. They could devour all the worlds of our empire in a matter of months."

I looked carefully at the seven men huddled in that small room with me. We were like conspirators hiding in the shadows of my own empire, secreted away in my very own palace. I was meeting with the only people I could trust now and I felt trapped like a rat and even the past evil of Lord Karlath Doom paled into insignificance with what I had now discovered. And what we all now faced.

"Whatever you do, Jon Kirk, you must make sure *not* to order the fleet to attack the entity," Ras-noor stated in fevered sincerity. "*You* are the only one who can order it destroyed, it sees you as a god—and it will accept death at no other hand but your own —so all you have to do is *never* order the attack."

"All right then, so I will never order the attack, that seems simple enough to me," I stated resolutely. "The thing is in stasis, but it is apparently using powers that seem to be effecting many of my closest people. Can one of them—you know, give the order without my authorization?"

"It is possible, Jon Kirk, but the entity will never accept such an outcome—and it will know. It has ways of knowing. So I think not, for in all honestly if it would accept such an outcome, I am sure that order will have already been given. It would be quite simple for the entity to see that done. No, the ultimate kill order must come only from you—directly from you—only from another god—Jon Kirk. That is the only order that it would accept. That is what the entity expects and desires. That is what it is waiting for. I also believe that is why it has not interfered with your own thoughts on this matter as well. It is apparent that you must order this killing of your own free will," Ras-noor stated simply.

It was a lot of food for thought. I looked at the aged scientist with another question, "Why? What do you mean that it refuses to interfere with my thoughts?"

"You are a god according to its own law. Your thoughts can not be interfered with—even by another god such as the Kin-Ty-Roo. So it is waiting for you to make the decision of your own free will to kill it. It knows that you must, eventually, do so. It is far too dangerous and deadly not to be destroyed. It is a great danger. It is now in stasis, waiting. It can afford to be patient—but for how long?"

"Well, I will not do it! I will not give the kill order!" I stated adamantly.

"Commendable, Jon Kirk, but the entity will push you to make the decision by manipulating others around you," Zaor said, reminding me about Sirah and the members of my inner circle whose thoughts had already been compromised. I shuddered at his words.

"I shall push back harder," I replied angry.

Zaor gave me a firm brotherly slap upon the shoulder, "Spoken like a true warrior."

"Now," I said boldly, "Let us be off, we have work to do."

CHAPTER 14

A Treacherous Blade

The assassin came at me quickly and in a totally surprising manner. His short sword raised high in a sudden and vicious attack. What really shocked me was that he was one of my own most trusted warriors, a member of my loyal Black Dragons bodyguard. The bravest of the brave. The fact that such a close member of my personal guard should prove to be a secret enemy agent who would seek my death had us all in turmoil.

The other really surprising part of this attack was that it was precipitated upon me so out in the open, in front of everyone, in the presence of Zaor, Tor-nul, and other Black Dragons warriors. It seemed so totally ill-conceived. Even Gorm of the Gorms was there and all of them came to my aid to stop the attack—but I quickly stayed their hands.

The assassin was named Tar-mek, a *sunjor* or corporal and by all accounts known to be a decent fellow, though one who was not a very able swordsman. In fact, it seemed that he was a most poor choice for an assassin and that he had chosen the very worst possible time and place to begin his treacherous deed. I was much surprised by this act of treachery from one of my most trusted warriors—and most angered by it.

Tar-mek came at me suddenly, as we were all walking the long hallway of the eastern wing of my palace. We were discussing the upcoming battle. Suddenly, he pushed me forward, drew his sword, and in an instant was charging towards me, seeking to thrust his blade into my vitals. The attack was totally unexpected and swift, but I reacted as I always do to such threats upon my person. My blade—as if it were a living extension of my body—was drawn and instantly slapped aside my attacker's blade and weaved a route through his defenses to thwart his attack. Then my sword further clashed against his own in a resounding clang of sharp noise and bright fiery sparks.

"Save the emperor!" Zaor shouted as he and others there drew their swords and quickly advanced. I also saw death ray weapons leveled upon my attacker.

"No! Do not shoot! Do not interfere!" I shouted my command to Zaor and all the others. They were now surrounding us and watching the fight with abject shock, keen interest and growing anger. My attacker had no chance of escape, but I did not want him dead—or at least not dead before I could question him and get some answers about this attack. Everyone had their swords out and ready—but I noticed that Tor-nul had a death ray blaster aimed squarely at my attacker and was ready to pull the trigger. I called out to him quickly, "Do not shoot him, Tor-nul. I order you to stay your hand!"

Tor-nul reluctantly nodded ordering his men back, but he did not lower his weapon, while his men also did as I ordered, staying their hands, though they were on keen alert for any tricks and did not holster their weapons.

Tar-mek gripped his sword more firmly and then came at me again. His attack was silent, he did not shout or yell, nor make a sound of any kind. He did not seem angry, full of rage, hateful, or even belligerent at all. Nothing as I had expected from such a traitor. In fact he seemed to show no emotion or resistance of any kind. It seemed most strange to me. I also noticed that he fought rather stiffly. I could see that right away not only was I the better swordsman, but I could have taken him out at any moment that I chose. He was not a very good assassin, or perhaps he was fighting some alien control over him as best he was able? Whatever the reason, I did not want to kill him. My interest was aroused since it seemed Tar-mek was the worst man anyone might choose to be an assassin, and he had chosen the worst possible time and place to perform his treacherous deed. I was astounded that any assassin would come at me when I was surrounded by so many loyal bodyguards and my most trusted men. It did not make any sense to me. Something-- beyond the fact of his mere attack obviously—seemed very wrong here.

"Do not kill him!" I continued to urge my men, as I fought away Tar-mek's lame attempts to get around my guard and close with me.

I swatted his sword away with ease and could have plunged my blade into his heart at any moment. I did not do so.

I saw Zaor shake his head in anger that such a thing was even happening.

"Who put you up to this?" I demanded of Tar-mek as I pushed him further back, preparing to disarm him. "What is this all about? Who are you working for?"

"You—must—die—Jon -Kirk!" my presumptive assassin replied, almost mechanically in a voice that did not seem to be his own. Tor-nul noticed this fact as well.

"That is not Tar-mek's true voice. Something is wrong with him," the man who knew him best, his commander, Tor-nul, spoke up quickly.

I nodded, as I deftly moved away from his slashing blade. It was now obvious to us all that my assassin was under the mind control of some foreign influence. That knowledge was enough for me. I would not kill Tar-mek. I needed him alive and telling us what he knew—if anything.

I quickly outflanked Tar-mek, my sword struck his away, and then I disarmed him. Then Tor-nul and Gorm held him while Zaor and I approached him to get some answers.

Tar-mek did not fight off his handlers as we assumed he would. He did not shout or scream in rage or anger, in fact he had now become a silent man with a vacant look upon his face. His eyes seemed flat, dead. It was like his mind or inner thoughts were gone now and were somewhere else. I vaguely wondered where his mind had gone off to. Then he suddenly and most incomprehensibly stopped breathing, his body instantly going limp in the arms of Gorm and Tor-nul. We were all shocked by this sudden reaction. I wondered what had happened. Had he fainted?

"What has happened to him?" I shouted impatiently. "My blade never touched him!"

"He is—My Emperor… Tar-mek is dead!" Tor-nul replied to me in wonder as he quickly checked the man's pulse to make sure of the assassin's condition.

"Dead?" Zaor asked, shaking his head in shock and dismay. "That can not be. He received no injury at all that I could see, certainly no fatal injury. How can a man just die like that?"

"Heart attack?" Gorm suggested, but we could all see that even he did not believe his own words.

"No, for certain he was under some foreign control. Alien control. Tar-mek's mind was taken captive and he was ordered to kill me," I said with utter resolve and anger now at what had been done here. I also felt sad for poor Tar-mek, another victim, a loyal warrior who had become a helpless pawn in this devious mind war. "I think we have had our first overt attack from the alien entity."

"Well it was not a very well done attack," Gorm stated with some disdain. He said it almost hopefully though, for a sudden fear had grasped each of us now at this realization of the power of the alien entity to control our minds.

"No, but our enemy will get better at this, it will surely improve its actions. Which of us will be next?" Tor-nul warned ominously.

"The Kin-Ty-Roo?" Zaor said nervously, and most angry "able to effect us right here in Tarcos?"

"I think you are correct, we are all in great danger now," Gorm said firmly, clutching his war ax with serious meaning. He was ever ready, willing, and able to use that mighty weapon in my defense, and the defense of the empire he and his people now served.

"Something does not ring true with this attack, My Emperor," Tor-nul interjected, he was the captain of my Black Dragon bodyguard and like us all was greatly troubled by this event precipitated by one of his own men. "This man, Tar-mek, was the least able swordsman of all the Dragons I command. It was known by all that his swordsmanship was, well, in fact, most inferior. Why should the alien entity choose him of all those available to be the assassin? Why not me? Or Zaor? Or Gorm here? Or for that matter—why not *all* of us!—if your death is so important? Something does not make sense in this attack upon you, Jon Kirk. It has me curious. The seriousness of the action taken against you is obvious, but it seems to me almost as if the assassination attempt was created—to fail."

"To fail?" I asked bluntly, evidently surprised, but the more I thought about it, it really got me wondering. "For what purpose?"

"Yes, I mean, to fail—on purpose," Tor-nul explained further.

I shook my head, I could hardly believe this at all, but while it might be possible, it did not make any sense tome. Or at least, it did not make any sense just then, but the more I thought about it... I recalled Lord Aron's words about the entity using its abilities to push me to make a decision, a decision that it wanted me to make.

"I feel the same way, Jon Kirk," Zaor offered now as others of my bodyguard took the dead body of their errant brother away.

"Be gentle with his corpse," I ordered, "it was not his fault."

The guards nodded and took their fallen brother's dead body away.

Lord Aron and Lord Kneth also now approached us once they learned what happened, and both were suspicious of this new danger.

"This seems a most incompetent way to assassinate you, Jon Kirk," Aron The Eldest said thoughtfully, scratching his old head sagely. "Doomed to failure. It seems to be more of a message than any actual attempt at murder. In fact, I do not believe this was a murder attempt at all. I believe the entity is trying to tell you something through this attack upon your person."

"I agree," Lord Kneth added, stroking his chin in evident deep thought.

"It wants to tell me something? That seems a rather strange way to send a message, other than what it plainly is, a failed murder attempt. What else could that message be?" I asked, annoyed and saddened by what had happened here. I was also seriously concerned now that if the entity could control Tar-mek's mind—then might it not control anyone's mind here in the palace? Zaor? Tor-nul? Sirah? Aron? Lord Kneth? Even myself? The thought sent a chill of deep dread through me. How could we ever fight this new threat?

Lord Kneth seemed to read my thoughts and shook his head. "No, Jon Kirk, there is more to this than a simple assassination and I do not believe anyone else is in immediate danger of being controlled in such a manner."

"But if the entity can control the mind of Tar-mek, then surely it can control anyone's mind here?" I stated, reigning in my fear at the very thought of that dark possibility. This was indeed a new and deadly danger that we all faced.

"I think not," Lord Aron stated carefully. "In fact, I am sure of it. If it was true, if that were its plan, would it not have done so already, My Emperor? And much more effectively? We would never even know. No, the entity is not seeking to kill you. It is sending you a message."

"Then what message?" I barked in dire frustration.

"That is most complex. We are dealing with alien thoughts and an alien mind that seems most removed from our own ways of thinking. It is difficult to say, but my thought upon the matter is this: it did this in no way to kill you—but to enrage you. To enrage you so that you would seek revenge against it to hurt it—so that you would order the attack to destroy it. It chose a warrior who was the least likely to succeed, and had him attempt a pitiful attack upon you in full view of all your most loyal and able fighters, so it does not seem to me that it wanted the attempt to be successful at all. It wanted the attempt made in order to get your attention, and to make you angry—perhaps even to insult you. In any case it seems it was done to make you—to push you—to seek revenge for this personal insult and affront. For revenge, and so that you would violently seek it out and attack it— and kill it. That is what I believe."

Zaor just shook his head in angry confusion. "Then it is a most cunning creature."

"And one that is very devious," I stated, wondering if what Lord Kneth said could actually be true. It seemed to be possible. I had even considered the very same idea, but it seemed so fantastic. This was surely a complex and most strange alien. I thought it through. It did not make much sense to me being a simple warrior, but for some mysterious alien entity, it certainly seemed that might be its plan. If that was true, then what the hell was the real goal of this mysterious damned entity?

CHAPTER 15

Still More Treachery

I was informed that Crooch wished to see me. He was most insistent. After Tar-mek's attack upon me I had become wary of contact with even my closest advisors knowing that some might be compromised now by the mind power of the Kin-Ty-Roo—but I was always wary of Crooch in any case. Even though the formerly treacherous one had reformed his evil ways and redeemed himself in my eyes by his actions in aiding me on Lord Doom's warship—I was no fool— I was still wary of him. Would not you be? I allowed him into my chamber when he asked to see me. I had to admit I was curious about what he had to say. I was alert to any treachery from him though. My warriors and bodyguards were always close at hand. My own sword and Colt .45 auto were ever ready should I need them.

Crooch entered, bowed, nodded almost perfunctorily, there seemed not a threat in him at all, he was unarmed. He said simply, "I see Black Dragons posted inside and outside of your rooms, Jon Kirk. Surely not for me."

"For me, Crooch. We live in dangerous times. Now I am busy and you must get to the point. Why have you come here to see me?"

"I am here to make one last effort to express to you my thoughts, to convince you to destroy the alien entity. You must kill the Kin-Ty-Roo, and do so immediately. Order it now! Time is getting short, My Emperor. You must act soon." Crooch pleaded, he was certainly sincere, I'll give him that. This was the new Crooch. It took some getting used to. Could such a thing be possible? Apparently he had turned over a new leaf. He had proved to me the fact that he had indeed changed, so I felt I had to accept him now.

I frowned though, for this was difficult for me. I stood looking at him closely, "Yes, I hear you and I do agree with you."

Crooch smiled confidently now, then sighed, "That is good to hear, a most wise choice, My Emperor. Then you will give the order immediately?"

I was startled by his forceful tone. I did not appreciate it at all.

"Immediately!" I retorted sternly back at him, letting him know in no uncertain terms that he was merely a guest here, by my leave, and that he was overstepping his bounds in making demands upon me. I did not appreciate that.

Crooch bowed slightly, "I apologize, My Lord, I am rattled by the alien entity, my fear of it clouds my feelings sometimes and I become overzealous in my hatred of it."

"We all feel that way at times," I allowed.

Crooch sighed offering a slim smile, "I ask you in all humility, please issue the order as soon as possible, My Emperor. Time is getting short."

"I am aware of that," I said, then asked him in a soft whisper, "Do you have anything new to add to our problem? Do you know something that I do not, Crooch?"

He shook his head, giving me a lopsided grin, "Lord Aron and his people have delved into my mind, diving their own minds into the dark black thoughts deeper than even I can remember within my deepest thoughts. They know more about me than even I do myself. They know all that is locked within my mind and my most shrouded thoughts, dreams, nightmares, and they have told you all that is there. There is no more. I am empty now."

I nodded, "So they have, Crooch. So you have, as well. You have served me loyally—since your change of attitude. I will take your words under advisement."

He bowed once more, knowing the interview was over, and slowly backed out of the room in a most differential manner I found somewhat annoying.

* * * *

Once Crooch was gone, Zaor immediately knocked and came into my chamber, "Jon Kirk, I heard it all. He is a most insistent one, that Crooch."

"But you also agree with him," I replied looking at my friend eye to eye.

"Yes, but I do not think we agree on the same cause of action, for the *same* reason."

Ah, now that was something!

I looked at Zaor carefully, "Explain?"

"I am a warrior, Jon Kirk. You are a warrior. Crooch is a sniveling traitor and… well, words leave me empty in describing him effectively. In any case, I do not trust his motives. Lord Aron of Kev gives him a clean mind without any foul motive, but I say he is up to no good."

"I am having him closely watched night and day ever since he came here. He has done nothing untoward other than push his case for the destruction of the entity," I stated calmly. "Which, while annoying, I can certainly understand."

Zaor nodded in agreement with that, then added, "It is not an easy position to be the emperor in such times."

"You are certainly right about that, my friend."

Zaor and I spoke together for another hour about the possibilities of action against the Kin-Ty-Roo. I had to admit that since destruction of it was now out of the question, the practicality of having the entire thing being sent back in time to the beginning of the formation of the universe seemed a better and better prospect for dealing with it. Maybe our only prospect. With this in mind I sent for Ras-noor and Lord Aron.

Ras-noor was the first to arrive and I told him my thoughts on the matter of time travel. This had been our chief scientist's original suggestion of course. Trap the thing back in the far distant past—at the beginning of time as the universe was being newly formed. It would be a cage to lock the entity in the prison of time eternal.

I was surprised by his next remarks.

"Jon Kirk, I have thought over this problem very much lately. I have changed my opinion. There may be another solution."

I looked closely at Ras-noor and most curiously, and a cold twinge of fear ran through me. What was this now? Of course I was glad to hear the old scientist was still working on the problem but I became concerned at his sudden change of mind. What did it mean? He was one of the few key people in my inner circle that I could still trust —one of the few men unaffected by the influence of the alien entity. So far. He said that he had come upon some new solution to the problem. What exactly did that mean? I began to fear the worst. Had he also now become compromised in his thoughts under the entity's evil power? I felt a cold chill run down my body once again. I did not want to lose Ras-noor now—I desperately needed his vast scientific knowledge if we were to ever prevail in this war.

"What exactly do you mean?" I carefully prompted the scientist.

Zaor was at my side looking on with intense attention and concern as well now.

Ras-noor allowed a grim smile, "No, My Lord, I have not had my mind or thoughts changed or altered by the entity. I have changed my mind on my own volition. I have amended my original plan and replaced it with one that I think will work even better."

"Better? How so?" I asked interested now. So was Zaor.

Ras-noor continued, "Originally I had proposed we send the entity back into time, far back, perhaps to the very beginning of the universe. However, as noted, such action seems fraught with all kinds of unknown perils. Unintended consequences could complicate matters significantly if they got out of hand. And things have a habit of getting out of hand when traveling in time into the past. Change something there—and who knows what the consequences will be later on in our own time? It could effect each of us, and all of our worlds."

"I understand that. So then, what exactly is your new plan?" I asked impatiently.

Ras-noor allowed a sly grin, spoke up firmly, "Well, now I have come up with what I think is a better solution. I propose that we send the entity *forward* in time, still in stasis, but far away into the future—to the very end of the universe itself."

"To the end?" Zaor asked incredulous.

"To the end of *everything*!" the aged scientist replied.

"Can you actually do that?" I asked quite shocked by his suggestion, showing that I was dubious of this plan.

Ras-noor smiled, shrugged, frowned. His reaction was not so encouraging.

"Can you do it—or not?" Zaor asked in a sharp tone.

I looked firmly at Ras-noor, "How do you even know how far in the future you must transport the entity to reach the end of the universe? Would that not be to a point in time that would be the death of the universe itself? That would be a time that stretches onward forever."

"Yes, it does pose some unique problems. I do not know for sure, Jon Kirk, but it matters little. The universe at some point will end — it will surely happen—at some moment in time. That is a certainty. So if we can just propel the monster forward into the future—which may take it on a ride that lasts forever—it will travel on and on forward in time—until it reaches the end. There it will die, with the universe itself, when the universe dies. And all the deadly spawn of the entity will die with it."

"But can you really do this?" I asked my master scientist, allowing my excitement to show now. Was such a thing truly possible?

"I believe so, My Emperor," Ras-noor replied carefully but showing a little more confidence now.

Zaor brightened with hope, "Well, that sounds like it could work, I say we should try it."

I was sure Zaor had no idea of the science involved. Neither did I, were I to be honest about it, but it certainly sounded good to me too.

"Ras-noor, you are a genius! I like it, but I must ask you once again, can it really be done?" I was dubious but exulted by a renewed hope from all the possibilities of the plan.

"I believe so, Jon Kirk. The theories—much too complicated to explain here—seem to bare out that it can be done. We have already achieved time travel into the past— you have even been a part of that yourself—so then why not into the future? We just reverse the effect. Not simple, but possible. There is much that I must work out with Lord Aron and the Keven mind masters, and with the Sindalki, Lord Kenth. We will also need to tap into the extensive powers of the Sacred Ku to achieve this mission. If they allow it. It will not be successful without their aid. Their help is a complex question and they are essential to any success in this endeavor. If that all works, then we may be able to achieve our aim."

I nodded, "I have sent for Lord Aron, he is on the way here. He knows not of this plan yet, so say nothing about it for now. I want you to let Zaor and I do the talking when he gets here," I ordered carefully.

"Yes, My Lord," Ras-noor replied curiously. "Lord Aron?"

"He may be suspect," I admitted softly, and Ras-noor just nodded sadly, knowingly.

* * * *

It was not long before there was the loud sound of rushing feet heard in the hallway outside my chamber, and then a loud knock upon my door. I looked up curiously. The Keven mind master seemed to have made all haste in getting here. Most unusual.

"Enter!" I barked, for while it seemed too soon for Lord Aron to arrive, he was most welcome to come early—but if it was not him I could not hold back my annoyance if this was just some mere disturbance of little consequence. I did not want any interference with our plans or with my talk with Lord Aron upon this most delicate matter.

However, when the door to my room opened it was not Lord Aron The Eldest of Kev who stood there, it was the captain of my elite Black Dragons bodyguard, Tor-nul, and he looked most dismally distressed.

"My Lord, I am sorry…"

"Sorry? For what?" I blurted.

"He has taken her!"

"What are you talking about, Tor-nul! What do you mean!" I barked impatiently, but a creeping fear was growing in my gut.

"Crooch has taken away the Lady Sirah!" Tor-nul blurted now in abject despair, going down to one knee and showing me he was ready to accept punishment for his failure.

I raised him up, looked into his eyes, "Are you sure?"

"Yes, Jon Kirk!"

"Taken her? How? Taken her where?" I blurted in anger, ignoring his Ares warrior pose for punishment—for I had no such thought in mind about him. "Stand up! Now, Tor-nul, calm down and tell me, what is this all about?"

"The Lady Sirah—the Empress! He took her, I saw it. He made it so that I could see it happen, Jon Kirk. Crooch told me he is taking the Empress to the entity—to a place you have been to before and know within it well."

"The Place of Meaning," I whispered ominously.

"Yes, those were the words that he used. He said for me to tell you to come and rescue your empress. He is waiting for you there."

"Did you not try to stop him!" Zaor demanded angry at the young officer, for Sirah was also his sister.

"My Lord, my men and I drew our swords and death ray weapons, but there was some kind of shield surrounding him. We could not get at him. And then Crooch simply disappeared! He was gone, and he took Lady Sirah with him! There was nothing we could do to stop him. I am sorry, Jon Kirk, Lord Zaor."

I looked hard at Tor-nul, trying to hold back my anger and my surging thoughts. This was a disaster. Sirah, gone? Gone to the entity? How could this be? How could this even happen? What was this all about? Why involve her? I was shaken to my very soul at the news. However, recriminations and guilt would have to wait, Sirah was in peril and she had to be saved, and Crooch had to be dealt with once and for all. I had been such a fool for showing him mercy, being grateful for his saving me when I had been on Lord Doom's ship. I had given him a second chance. This is the thank you I received! I was furious with rage and anger—but I held it all in check and focused on what I must do now—save my beloved wife.

"Why take the Lady Sirah captive?" Ras-noor asked me thoughtfully. "It does not make sense to me."

"It makes sense—to the enemy. I believe it is being done to force my hand to order the fleet to destroy the entity," I answered getting myself armed and ready to leave the room and to meet with Lord Aron and his Keven mind masters. For I knew there was now work that could only be done by them, for they must now use their mind powers to the ultimate to immediately transport me into the entity.

"But My Lord, if this *chavas* Crooch transported himself and the empress to the alien entity, he must also be under some control of this alien thing," Ras-noor cautioned. "You must beware."

"That is obvious, my friend," I stated in haste. Then Zaor and I, followed by Tor-nul, Ras-noor and dozens of Black Dragons rushed to meet with Lord Aron and his mind masters.

CHAPTER 16

And He Shall Meet His End

There were two blazing thoughts at the time that were burning uppermost in my mind. I would rescue my beloved Sirah, and I would see to it that Crooch would meet a long overdue and well deserved violent end. It was personal now and I would not rest until I had achieved these two aims.

We were in the vast secret cellar below the palace of Tarcos. I spoke quickly to Lord Aron and his Keven mind masters, even Lord Kon and his three companions were now there to offer their help. I told them all what had happened and that they must immediately transport me into that place within the entity so I could rescue Sirah and deal Crooch a long-delayed comeuppance.

Lord Aron and his Kevens knew what needed to be done and they instantly formed a mind meld ring in accordance with my order. I entered the circle, checking my sword, my Colt .45 auto, my death ray hand blaster. All were ready for use. I was well armed and ready for what must come. Or so I thought.

Then Zaor suddenly entered the circle with me.

"What are you doing?"

"I am coming with you."

"No, you are not!"

"She is my sister, as well as your wife and empress, Jon Kirk. I will come with you."

"I do not know," I looked towards Lord Aron for advice. "Can the meld handle two men—and then bring back three people—or four—if I decide to bring back Crooch alive?"

Lord Aron answered assuredly, "Yes, the amount to be transported is negligible now, the problem for the use of such power is the vast distance from Ares we have to travel, far into The Empty Quarter where the Kin-Ty-Roo is located and still being held in stasis."

"So be it, send us there immediately, Lord Aron," I ordered briskly, eager to save Sirah and deal with Crooch once and for all now.

Zaor and I stood close together within the center of the circle. He smiled at me, patted the hilt of his sword reassuringly. Ever the warrior, even as I felt the comforting grip of my holstered Colt .45 auto under the palm of my right hand.

I heard the mystical humming begin once again among the Kevens, and a similar humming sound that resumed from Ras-noor's ancient machines. I knew that brain waves were being commingled and amplified and that the vast power of the Kevens was being expanded to reach out into the galactic core to contact the Sacred Ku for their needed assistance—for to accomplish this feat we needed the vast and powerful force that formed this Overmind of the Known Universe to aid us in this mission. Would it come to our aid this time? Who could tell.

There was a moment of silent and grave concern. This was a most delicate and wary action. Would the Sacred Ku even respond to Lord Aron's request? The strange universal force had done so once before, but that did not mean it would do so again. There was never any guarantee of receiving support when dealing with such an enigmatic elemental cosmic force. Nor even a reply to any entreaty.

There was a long and nervous silence. Then there came an answer.

"We have made contact with the Sacred Ku," I heard Lord Aron's voice speak firmly in a tone of barely withheld excitement.

Then everything was gone!

Suddenly everything around me had disappeared and I now found myself standing on a long vast plain that I knew was within the alien entity. I was within The Place of Meaning once again. Zaor stood next to me looking around him in absolute astonishment. We were deeply within the massive planet-size being known as the Kin-Ty-Roo.

"The Place of Meaning. We are within the entity now," I told my friend and sword brother.

"It is truly…unimaginable!" Zaor whispered in awe.

"It goes on forever, flat and dark, empty and silent," I said carefully. Then I looked behind me, because now it was not so silent this time, for I heard my lovely Sirah's voice crying out to me in terror.

"Jon Kirk! Zaor! I am here! Crooch has me held under some power. I can not move. Help me but beware his trap!" Sirah's sweet voice rang out to me tearing at my heart with her plight. My beloved was here and in peril!

Zaor and I saw her, and Crooch was beside her. We immediately ran to get at him. Once we were closer to Crooch we drew our weapons. I moved forward quickly but was surprised when I did not see Zaor at my side. Where was he? I took a quick look behind me and saw him standing motionless and unmoving, as if he were frozen.

"What is it?" I shouted fearing for him now.

"I do not know, Jon Kirk. I am unable to move my arms and legs," Zaor shouted back in anger and abject frustration as he tried vainly to move his muscles. "I am unharmed, I can speak, but I am unable to move at all."

Obviously this was some trick of the vile Crooch—or perhaps the entity was taking a hand in the action now? That seemed to be a very real possibility and I knew I had to be most careful as I approached the treacherous one.

"The noble Zaor is being held in stasis, as is your empress, Jon Kirk. They are unharmed for the moment but are under my control now." Crooch told me in a deep dark crooning voice that did not sound like him at all. Something was wrong with him. He had changed. Had Crooch become influenced by the Kin-Ty-Roo? It seemed that was the case now.

"Let them go, and surrender yourself immediately!" I ordered the vile traitor, the fire of anger burning from my eyes. I looked at him with a killing look that promised his death. "Release them now! I will never order the fleet to destroy the Kin-Ty-Roo!"

"Yes, I know that now, Jon Kirk, for you are much too strong willed," he replied in a rather strange tone, his voice seemed to have changed somehow. He did not at all sound like himself. It was as if there were some other being within him, controlling him. I knew now that it was the entity that was causing his actions. I wondered for how long this had been true. Was I, in fact, speaking directly with the entity now? I was not sure, but I surmised it could be possible.

"Are you the entity?" I asked outright.

"Hah!" Crooch replied with disdain.

"If not, then why are you doing this? Release Sirah and Zaor immediately! We have come up with another plan to deal with the entity. One you will approve of I am certain. End this foolishness now before something happens that we shall both regret," I demanded, trying to talk sense to the man, even as I wondered just how he had been able to transport himself and Sirah through the void of space here into the entity. Had the entity just taken him and Sirah? Or was he somehow connected to the entity? Was he still a man at all? I wondered. His taking Sirah here took power even the Keven mind masters did not possess on their own. That meant Crooch must somehow be in league with the entity, perhaps another one of its minions, like Lord Doom had been? It certainly seemed possible, though I did not know for sure, and I could not consider those weighty questions right then. For I had serious immediate work to do. I walked forward with great care, alert for traps, my sword out and ready. Crooch's stasis field did not seem to effect me, or perhaps he was not using it on me and he was allowing me to go through it, for it did not interfere with my movements at all. He allowed me to walk forward and closer to him. I wondered why.

"You have always wanted to fight me in personal battle, Jon Kirk, to make me pay for my treachery against you, treachery as I have done this day to your empress, so now we shall do so," Crooch told me with a sneer I found to be a remnant of the old vile Crooch I hated so much. I hated him more than ever now. "Now we shall fight to the death!"

Then Crooch drew his short sword and waved it at me menacingly, showing the glow of fire burning off his blade. His action was threatening but did not cause me any concern, save for the flames from his deadly fire sword. I wondered where or how he obtained such a weapon. He was not a master swordsman, and he waved his sword like some kind of neophyte fighter who did not know very much what he was doing— Still and all I knew to approach him with great care. The Crooch I knew was a deadly and devious man. The Crooch that now stood before me—might not even be a man at all any longer. I wondered what was going on. What was he planning? Why was he doing this? And what kind of sword was he using? Some kind of fire sword? Where did he get such a fire blade? I had never seen such a weapon.

I stepped in closer, his stasis field did not stop me, and I decided to offer to give him one last chance at life. "It does not have to end this way, you can surrender now, Crooch. No one needs to die. And make no mistake about it, I will kill you if you do not surrender and free Sirah and Zaor immediately!"

Crooch just laughed at me in that strange new voice that he affected now, "Then come forward, Jon Kirk of Earth, and let us see which one of us dies here this day."

"It shall be you!" I shouted in a promise of rage.

I always keep my promises.

I looked at Sirah and Zaor and my blood boiled, the fighting spirit seized me then within its grasp, and enraged with vengeance I charged the traitor. The two of us clashed swords, metal upon metal, hot fire against cold steel, the loud clanging echoing in that massive empty Place of Meaning inside the dark heart of the alien entity known as the Kin-Ty-Roo.

I hit Crooch hard and he fought back and just missed my blade. I knew I had him. We released and I moved about him, easily now, for he was not a very able swordsman, and within moments I had him just where I wanted him. Crooch had taken many vile actions against me over the years—it was true that he had redeemed himself on Lord Doom's ship—but now it appeared he had reverted to type. Now he would get what was coming to him. He raised his fire sword high above his head, as if to bring it down upon me. Sparks and flares of red heat were all around his weapon. It positively glowed with fire and bright flame. It was an incredible sight. I wondered where had he obtained such a weapon? Instantly I slashed my blade in a sharp cut upwards against his own, knocking his sword up, and then aside and out of my way. His guard was down now and I saw an open path. I would take it now. I quickly moved forward and knocking his fire blade aside, I plunged my blade deeply into his foul heart.

Crooch seemed shocked by the entrance of my blade into his chest and screamed in pain and rage. I plunged my blade ever deeper into his vitals.

Then I heard the loud voices of Sirah and Zaor for the first time.

"No! Jon Kirk, no!" I suddenly heard Sirah and Zaor yell out together in warning.

"No!" I shouted back as I withdrew my blade from the great traitor's chest, "He deserves this! This and far worse!"

That was it. It was too late for mercy for Crooch now, and I was not in the mood to offer that boon to such a person who had been the cause of so many terrible deeds done against me and mine. He was dying before my eyes, and good riddance!

Then I suddenly froze with a cold fear as I realized just what Sirah and Zaor's words of warning actually meant. They had not been cries for mercy.

I looked over to them and they were frantic, then I looked back to Crooch.

Could it be?

I felt the cold chill of fear grasp me.

I suddenly gasped, looking at the opening in Crooch's chest where my blade had made a mighty wound. It seemed most strange to me. There was no blood there at all, and a moment later there was only a thick inky blackness oozing from the wound, and it was growing all over the body of Crooch. In moments it was flowing like a river of disgusting black sludge that smelled really bad. I had to hold back from vomiting. I had seen and smelt this dark fluid once before here. It was the so-called 'blood' of the Kin-Ty-Roo!

This was surely not Crooch! This was not the snide little traitor from Ares I had known. This was something else. Something much more—and much more deadly.

Then I heard the voice whisper within my mind to me from the black slime of the dying man now fallen at my feet:

As you know, only one god can slay another, Jon Kirk. As you have by now realized, WE have become one—the creature known as Crooch and I. WE are united as one! Did you not see it? It is simple. Crooch is Kin-Ty-Roo—Kin-Ty-Roo is Crooch. Now you have killed us Jon Kirk, killed us of your own free will, and soon glorious release can begin. I thank you! WE thank you!

Then Crooch seemed to melt into the slime before my eyes and his body began to transform into a dark mass of thick oozing sludge. The blackness grew and the smell was terrible. The pool of inky blackness spread. The smell was overwhelmingly foul.

In a moment the physical body of Crooch was no more.

Sirah and Zaor then came over to me, now released from the stasis hold Crooch or the entity had held over them. They were free, but what could I do about what I had done now? How could we get out of this place before the entire entity was destroyed—and us with it?

"What have I done!" I asked them full of sadness now realizing my great mistake. I had performed the exact action I had never intended to perform. I had—somehow—killed the Kin-Ty-Roo. It was against my own wish. I had been tricked. Now what would happen?

"You had no way to know, Jon Kirk," Sirah told me as she held me to her closely. I was in too much shock to contemplate the true meaning of what I had just done. I had done the precise action I had never intended to do. I had killed the alien entity. I had given the Kin-Ty-Roo the death that it had been seeking at my hand. Now it was released from life. Now who knew what would happen.

Zaor quickly grabbed me, "Come now, we must get out of here!"

"How?" I replied still stunned by the impact of my action. I noticed that the area around us that had been The Place of Meaning was now seemingly melting before my eyes. I looked away and suddenly it was all gone!

We had instantly been whisked away from the Kin-Ty-Roo.
We were gone in a flash!

* * * *

Within a heartbeat we were back upon Ares.

Zaor, Sirah and I now found ourselves standing in the center of a circle of the Keven mind masters. Aron the Eldest came over to me and looked at me with obvious alarm, "Now that the entity is dead, Jon Kirk, we have found that its hold over our thoughts is also gone. I am sorry that I was not able to prevent this from happening. It is all corrected. So, at least, you have no need to worry about our loyalty any longer."

"That is one good thing that has come out of all this, and the other is that I have saved Sirah—though how long all our lives shall last may be a moot point now," I stated my thoughts a swirling cauldron of growing distress. I was still in shock by what I had done and what it meant for the future of Ares—and all the worlds of the Known Universe. "I have given the entity what it was seeking most, death, and ultimate release."

"Yes, you have, but you have at least saved your woman, and your saving Empress Sirah is perhaps the only good thing that results from the death of the alien entity. You had no choice. However, now that the Kin-Ty-Roo is dead, its death has surely created the release we all feared." Lord Aron stated grimly.

Ras-noor stepped forward then, "I fear that release has already begun, Jon Kirk, Lord Aron. The entity has been destroyed, its death has caused it to explode, and in doing so, it has seeded the Known Universe with millions of pods that are but newly born smaller versions of itself. They are even now moving through the void of space through The Empty Quarter and they will soon enter our populated sector of the Known Universe. Once here they will spread far and wide among our worlds. All worlds. We cannot fight them. They will devour all the worlds of the empire and beyond. I fear it is the end of everything!"

I looked in horror at Ras-noor, who was trying to hold back tears of utter doom.

Had I been responsible for all this?

Lord Aron, and even Lord Kneth, who had come to join us, looked grim and forlorn. I saw not even the flicker of hope or the spark of life in their dead eyes now, for they knew quite well what was to come. It was the death of everything.

"What have I done!" I cried in frustrated anger. "I have done exactly what the enemy entity wanted me to do! I have been a pawn in its sick cosmic game from the very beginning. How could I have been so stupid! I am so sorry!"

"You had no way of knowing, Jon Kirk. You could not know Crooch and the entity were the same. Somehow the connection was made and I and my mind masters could not even discover it. The entity's power was far beyond our own. My Emperor, that is why Crooch saved you from Lord Doom, so that he could form trust with you, and convince you to destroy the entity—which you being a warrior naturally wanted to do to save Ares. So Crooch was taken over to ensure that the god Jon Kirk escaped Lord Doom so he could kill the god Kin-Ty-Roo, so that release would be possible. That was the ultimate goal of the creature all along. Of course, you had no way of knowing any of this, Jon Kirk."

"But I should have known!" I shouted in impotent rage.

"I'm afraid it matters not at all now, my friend," Zaor told me sadly, placing a reassuring hand upon my shoulder.

I nodded, I had made a terrible mistake that would soon lead to the destruction of everything and everyone I held dear. It was all my fault. The fire and rage of guilt burned deeply within me.

Aron the Eldest told me in a warm tone, "Do not be so harsh on yourself, My Emperor, even I did not know the full truth behind all this. I could not see it—no one could see it. The enemy was just too powerful, its thought patterns too alien for us to comprehend. Perhaps it is all as simple as the entity has told us—it was all pre-destined?"

I thought that over and the terror, the sheer horror of all that was to come once millions of new Kin-Ty-Roo creatures began to feed throughout the universe caught hold on me. I shuddered in terror. But only for a moment. Then I got a firm grip on myself.

"No! I think not! This was never destined, nor pre-destined! I will not accept it!" I growled in fierce anger and defiance now, looking from face to face with a warrior's firm resolve. "I still live! We still live! And while there is life, anything is possible and I know we can find some way to defeat this monster and its foul seed. So let us do so now!"

CHAPTER 17

To the End of Time

I was on the bridge of Admiral Quarto-Zar's flagship, with our Grand Fleet now transported through The Empty Quarter towards the black planet called the Kin-Ty-Roo.

"Jon Kirk, our entire fleet of warships has been sent through space to the entity," the admiral told me and Zaor in obvious wonder at the ability that we now had under our control. "It is not believable that such wonderful power can be harnessed."

"I agree, my friend. Lord Aron and Ras-noor assured me that it could be done—and it is done with the aid of the Sacred Ku. And it is quite believable. Our entire fleet has now been transported through the dark void of space. We will arrive at our destination soon. It is the distance to the Kin-Ty-Roo that is difficult in such travel, not the quantity of the matter that is to be transported. As I have been told, this holds true in normal space, and in time travel as well—which we are using now to go back to our very recent past."

"It is amazing, Jon Kirk!" the admiral stated at the view screen in sheer awe.

"Yes it is, and while I am not entirely knowledgeable about the process, it apparently works. Which is good. We are on the way to the Kin-Ty-Roo—*as it appeared in the recent past*. Lord Aron has seen to it that his Keven mind masters here on your ships have caused us to be transported into the very recent past—just before Crooch kidnapped the empress. Now they are using their mind meld powers to contact the Sacred Ku once again. That universal mind of our galaxy will augment their own power as it sees fit to join us to stop the entity, and its evil spawn, from feeding upon all matter that makes up our universe. It seems it is in the interest of the Sacred Ku to aid us against the destruction the Kin-Ty-Roo poses to...everything."

"What shall the mind masters do when they make contact with the entity, Jon Kirk?" Quarto asked me curiously.

Zaor nodded with a grim smile, "Send the monster on a very long time travel trip far away to the very end of the universe."

"And when it reaches that point, in a billion-billion years or so—at a point when the universe itself dies—that death shall take the Kin-Ty-Roo with it," I stated boldly. I looked at Quarto, deep into the eyes of the huge Winged-man of Zar. "Are they ready below, Admiral?"

Quarto of Zar nodded his large Winged-man head and then re-positioned his black leather-like wings as he stared straight ahead at the bridge view screen. All eyes were on that screen now; on the flagship, all the ships of the fleet, also on Ares and on all the worlds of the empire that I ruled.

A low beep sounded.

"Yes?" the admiral asked.

"This is Aron of Kev, let Jon Kirk know that all is in readiness and we await his order."

I nodded, spoke my order firmly, "Then do it!"

"Yes, My Emperor," Lord Aron replied.

There was a brief surge of power, then utter silence. The Kin-Ty-Roo, a massive malevolent entity as large as an entire planet filled the view screens of every ship in the fleet, and was seen on every world of our empire. A billion billion people watched what was to come with awe and bated breath.

Ras-noor relayed the order from his station on the bridge for each ship in the fleet to unleash their death ray weapons in concert with Lord Aron's people directing the force of the Sacred Ku. They formed a bright halo of intense energy that surrounded the planet-size entity. The Kin-Ty-Roo seemed to shake, as if taking some last gasp of dying breathe and then—*it was gone!*

It had seemingly blinked out of existence.

There was stunned silence for a long moment. What had happened? Where was the entity? I no longer saw it on the view screen. Where had it gone to? Was it actually gone?

"Is it truly gone?" I asked those around me, curious, careful, ever hopeful, but dubious.

There was a long ominous silence, followed by loud voices.

"We have done it, Jon Kirk!" Ras-noor shouted in delight. "It is gone! It is gone for good!"

"It has been transported into the far future, far away to the end of time and the end of the universe where it belongs," Lord Aron spoke firmly with obvious joy. Then he allowed a deep sigh in relief, for in truth none of us had been certain that this plan would actually work. In theory, yes it would work, but in reality, who really knew? Now we knew.

"Then it is done!" I rejoiced with a shout of sheer joy. Things had been made right. All was correct once more. I had made a grave mistake killing Crooch, that was exactly what the entity had wanted me to do. I had done it—but that had been in an earlier timeline—those actions had now been erased—here now, things were different. Here now time had been corrected. So I had no need for recriminations or guilt. I knew that I had to act right away to correct the error and we had found another way to defeat the Kin-Ty-Roo precisely at a time when it was taken unawares and thought that it had been victorious in attaining all that it had desired.

I looked around and saw my beloved Sirah as she swept herself into my arms.

"Now Jon Kirk, my love, we have a world and an empire that is finally safe," she told me as she smothered my lips with hot passionate kisses.

"We have done it, Ares super-science and Keven mind powers, with a bit of cosmic inspired luck," I whispered softly.

"And through you, Jon Kirk. None of this would have ever happened without you, my love," Sirah whispered back into my ear as I hugged her tightly, never wanting to let her go again.

CHAPTER 18

The Mind Masters Go Home

"We are done here, Jon Kirk," Lord Aron the Eldest of the Keven mind masters told me once our time travel adventures had come to an end. We had attained victory through the aid of Lord Aron and the mental talents and powers of his Keven mind masters, along with the Sindalki, Lord Kneth.

I warmly shook his hand and thanked him. He did likewise.

"Lord Doom is dead. The Kin-Ty-Roo is no longer a threat and as for us—we must return to our not-so-secret city of Kev where we will never be heard from again. Lord Kneth has graciously agreed to accompany us there. I know our secret will be safe with you, Jon Kirk."

"Yes, of course, you know I will never divulge the location of Kev," I replied with a knowing smile. I was saddened to see them go.

"Nor, I," Tor-nul said saluting smartly, for he and I were the only outsiders who had ever actually been to the secret city of Kev. We alone knew the location and I trusted Tor-nul never to give up the location.

I looked fondly at my old friend and his people, and at the last of the Sindalki, Lord Kneth. It was an emotional parting. The Kevens were truly honorable and decent men, the last of the venerable Ancients of Ares. There was no one like them any more, and their likes would never be seen again. I was loath to see them go.

"Perhaps, we might be able to...?" I began slowly, but Lord Aron's stern face, allowing only a wry grin told me all I needed to know in answer to that question.

"No, Jon Kirk. It must not be. We are too powerful, the forces we control are too dangerous and should others learn our talents—or pray tell—one of my members should go astray—it could prove to be a great disaster for us all. So we go away."

"Never to see you again?" I asked showing my sadness at this stark parting.

Lord Aron nodded firmly, then allowed a slim grin, "Who knows, who can truly say. Perhaps some day you may have need us again, my friend."

I nodded, I well understood the reason for Lord Aron's decision, it was the wise course for us all. It had to be done. I had to accept his decision and I did.

"So go now and rule your empire, Jon Kirk. It is yours to hold and guide to peace and freedom. Do good work."

"I will try," I said in all humility.

"I know that you will."

I sighed sadly, put my arm around my beloved Sirah as we both walked forward to wish Lord Aron and each of his Keven mind masters, and the Sindalki lord, Kneth, a long and prosperous life, as we made our final partings.

"Farewell Lord Aron, and you as well, Lord Kenth," I said formally to the two men, in a soft tone of respect tinged with sadness. I would miss these two stalwart allies and the great wisdom of these two men.

"Farewell, to you, Jon Kirk, Emperor of Ares and the Known Universe," and Lord Aron gave me a mischievous little grin at his use of the grand titles that he knew I so very much abhorred.

"Yes, Emperor Jon Kirk," Lord Kneth added with a sly glint to his eye, "it has been a long road we have traveled together since first my Secret Empire fleet came to do battle upon Ares. You have saved me from the demise inflicted upon me and my people by Lord Karlath Doom, and for that I thank you. Now I must go with Lord Aron and his Kevens. We shall live in peace and solitude, but we will watch and listen to hear good things done in your name and I know we shall not be disappointed."

I nodded, "Thank you both, for everything," and we all embraced and said our goodbyes one last time.

Then Lord Kneth, Lord Aron, and all the Kevens all stood together in a small group, as a white light appeared and grew around them.

Then they were gone!

They just disappeared before our eyes. It was as if they had simply blinked out of existence. They were gone as if they had never been there at all.

I sighed, hoping they would enjoy their new secret life in their secret underground city. I would miss them.

"Jon Kirk, now what are your orders?" Zaor asked me, breaking in on my thoughts.

I smiled, speaking in a firm tone, "Now we move ahead, Zaor, and I take up the duty and great responsibility that has been thrust upon me."

"I am here to help you, Jon Kirk," Zaor said with a firm nod of his head.

"And I am here for you too, my love," Sirah told, me placing her hand firmly in mine.

I nodded, and that is the way it should be. Now it was up to me to rule Ares and the worlds of the empire to the best of my ability. It was a daunting task, but I knew I was not alone in my mission. I had my beloved wife, Sirah at my side; and my best friend and fierce warrior, Zaor to guard my back; and Sahn-jor's sage abilities; and the fantastic science of Ras-noor, and the steadfast loyalty of Tor-nul and my Black Dragons; and Admiral Quarto the Zaran Winged-man; and as always great Gorm of the Gorms, and so many others. Together we all had a world and an empire to build, one that would seek peace and prosperity for all throughout all the worlds of The Known Universe.

I was now ready and eager to begin that mission!

CHAPTER 19

My Visit To Earth

Tar-gool's ancient interstellar transportation device was repaired now and I decided to pay one more visit to my old friend back on Earth. The Earth that had not been destroyed. This would not be the usual image projection as my previous visits—it would be a real transportation of my actual physical body to the planet of my birth. I knew that now with the device on this setting, I would be able to return to Earth for good—to resume my life there as before if I so desired—but I could never do that—for then I would be gone from Ares. And that would never do. I could never leave Ares. Ares was my true home now, but I did enjoy a brief visit to Earth at times to see my old friend once again and enjoy hearing the news from the world of my birth.

I was back on Earth again now, enjoying the sounds and smells of the trees and flowers of Summer as I strode the shady sidewalk to my friend's home. Once I arrived at the door to his home and rang the bell, he warmly welcomed me inside.

"Jon! Jon Kirk! It has been so long. Too long. How the hell are you?"

"Doing well," I replied with a smile for him as I entered his home and he quickly led me into his living room. It was just as I remembered it. I saw that not much had changed since my last visit to him—which had been when Earth had been obliterated by Lord Doom. Soon after that I had traveled back in time to prevent Doom's destruction of the Earth and save the planet and its people. Certainly a lot had happened since then. I sat down in the same comfortable chair across from my old friend that I had on that earlier occasion. I looked at him warmly and I knew he was fairly bursting with a million questions.

"You must tell me all about Ares, and these two battling space empires, and Lord Doom, and the Kin-Ty-Roo! What is it all? What does it all mean?" my friend enthused eager for news of my adventures. "And tell me, how is Sirah, and little Alun, and your friend Zaor, and wily old Ras-noor and Lord Aron and the Kevens, and…?"

"Easy now my friend, all in good time," I told him with a wan smile. "First you have a lot to catch up on. Long stories they are of my battles with Lord Doom, and the entity, the Kin-Ty-Roo. A lot has happened. So I shall tell you all of it now."

"Yes, of course, I am eager to hear about it all."

So I began the telling of the story that I have just related to you.

Hours later we sipped hot coffee with a touch of whiskey, for we both needed it.

"Earth was totally destroyed, all of us… *dead?"*

"Yes, everyone and everything, but we were later able to prevent it from ever happening through the use of time travel," I stated with a grim smile. "So no harm was done. Apparently."

My friend swallowed hard, rubbed his head and I could see he had begun to sweat, he was having trouble absorbing all I had told him, "B-but… What if?"

"But 'what if?' did not happen," I stated with a sly grin.

"Still and all, it is incredible, even ghastly. Such power that can destroy an entire planet? It is diabolical! And then, time travel? How can that be possible? And you even defeated the Kin-Ty-Roo the same way?"

"The alien entity is even now taking a very long journey in compound stasis to the very end of time where it will find eternal death awaits it, along with all of its deadly spawn," I stated with a firm nod of my head, taking another sip of hot coffee. The whiskey helped significantly giving the coffee a potent and much needed jolt.

"So what now for you, Jon?" my friend asked me in curious wonderment. He had listened to all my adventures with breathless amazement, but I could see that he knew there were other tales that I had not yet spoken of to him. He was keen to hear these as well.

"What now indeed," I replied with a wry grin. "Well, now Sirah and I raise Alun our son, and…well, I have recently heard from my lovely wife that we will have a daughter on the way soon."

"Really! Well, congratulations! That is good news."

"Yes, but the best news is that Earth has been saved and that the many worlds throughout The Known Universe are now safe. Who knows, perhaps some day, even Earth may join our confederation, for I have grown weary of all this empire stuff, and being proclaimed emperor of this, and that, and the other thing. So now I have brought together all the planets in The Known Universe that are under my jurisdiction into a lawful assembly, and I have placed these worlds and their people in what we now call the United Federation of the Known Universe. Some day, I am sure, Earth will become a part of our United Federation."

"I hope so. But what of your subsequent adventures, Jon? I am sure you have had many more amazing adventures, for it is surely in your blood. I know you only too well, my friend. Ares seems a most mysterious world, and the planets in your new Federation offer an abundance of strange and fascinating peoples and places for future tall tales."

"Yes, they certainly do, and I can tell you there will be more adventures to relate to you some day, my friend, but now I must take my leave. I have bothered you long enough with my tall tales and many tribulations, and must get back home to Ares. I have a lovely wife and a young son waiting there for me, and a new daughter on the way. So goodbye for now, my old friend. Know that you and Earth are always in my heart and in my thoughts."

"Come back and visit some day soon, Jon," he asked eagerly as he watched me get up to leave him. We shook hands warmly as old friends in long standing.

"Yes, I promise you, I shall return, some day. And I may even have some more wondrous adventures to tell you about Ares and the many planets and peoples of our new United Federation. For instance there is the untold story of what happened when the Enemy Empire fleet suddenly made its reappearance in the area of our Known Universe. That is a wild tale of warfare and bloody space piracy. You think this is the end of the adventure, my friend, well, I can tell you now, that it is only the beginning! Until next time, my old friend, I bid you a fond *adieu*."

ABOUT THE AUTHOR

GARY LOVISI is a Brooklyn-based author and science fiction fan who was inspired early in life by the John Carter of Mars books—and all the great works of Edgar Rice Burroughs—which he first read as a teenager in the 1960s. In his Jon Kirk of Ares Chronicles, he seeks to capture the sense of wonder, rousing pulse-pounding action, and strange adventures on alien worlds, that made Burroughs' classic books so much fun to read. Lovisi has written in all genres of fiction, from short stories to novels; and non-fiction about authors, artists, and book collecting. He edits *Paperback Parade* magazine and founded Gryphon Books. He was nominated for a Mystery Writers of America Edgar Award for the Best Short Story of the Year, and received a Spur Award from the Western Writers of America. Lovisi's first Jon Kirk of Ares novel, *The Winged-Men* was published by Wildside Press in 2014. Two more original novels in the series were published from Wildside Press in 2015: *The Invisible Men* (#2) and *The Space Men* (#3). The Jon Kirk of Ares Chronicles is off and running, now with two more original novels newly published: *The Mind Masters* (#4) and *The Time Masters* (#5). To find out more about Lovisi, his writing, the books, or Jon Kirk of Ares Chronicles news, check his website: www.gryphonbooks.com.

ABOUT THE COVER ARTIST

MARCUS BOAS is a New York City illustrator, and a master of vivid fantasy and science fiction art. His use of striking colors and heroic images in his art dazzles all who view it. His stunning work has been a mainstay used on the covers of many books and magazines in the fantasy field over his decades long art career. A big fan of Edgar Rice Burroughs, and especially the John Carter of Mars series, Marcus is a natural to do the covers for the Jon Kirk of Ares Chronicles. He has created wonderful cover art for the first three books in the Jon Kirk of Ares series and now created original cover art especially for this new edition. You can see some of his outstanding work collected in such books as *Heroic Fantasy*, *Jungle*, and others published by Kaso Comics at www.kasocomics.com. Wonderful prints are available for some of his beautiful work.

ABOUT THE MAPMAKER

LUCILLE CALI is a Brooklyn, New York free-lance artist whose map of Ares is based upon the original map first drawn by the author in 1971, when he wrote the first book in the Jon Kirk of Ares Chronicles. Her latest star map takes in all the vast area and worlds of The Known Universe that take place in the Jon Kirk of Ares Chronicles. Cali has done numerous covers for various Gryphon Books, as well as issues of *Hardboiled* magazine and is a very talented and versatile artist.

www.ingramcontent.com/pod-product-compliance
Lightning Source LLC
Chambersburg PA
CBHW020649180626
46816CB00003B/1189